Praise for the Inspector DeKok ~~series~~

"Along with such peers as Ed McBain and Georges Simenon, [Baantjer] has created a long-running and uniformly engaging police series. They are smart, suspenseful, and better-crafted than most in the field."
—*Mystery Scene*

"Baantjer's laconic, rapid-fire storytelling has spun out a surprisingly complex web of mysteries."
—*Kirkus Reviews*

"DeKok is a careful, compassionate policeman in the tradition of Maigret; crime fans will enjoy this book."
—*Library Journal*

"DeKok's maverick personality certainly makes him a compassionate judge of other outsiders and an astute analyst of antisocial behavior."
—*The New York Times Book Review*

"It's easy to understand the appeal of Amsterdam police detective DeKok; he hides his intelligence behind a phlegmatic demeanor, like an old dog that lazes by the fireplace and only shows his teeth when the house is threatened."
—*The Los Angeles Times*

Other Inspector DeKok Mysteries
Available or Forthcoming from Speck Press

DeKok and the Geese of Death, #18
DeKok and Murder by Melody, #19
DeKok and the Death of a Clown, #20
DeKok and Murder by Installment, #22

DeKok and
Variations on Murder

Number 21 in the Inspector DeKok Series

by

A. C. Baantjer

Translated by H. G. Smittenaar

speck press
denver

Published by: *speck press,* speckpress.com

Book layout and design by: *CPG,* corvuspublishinggroup.com
Printed and bound in the United States of America

ISBN: 1-933108-04-5, ISBN13: 978-1-933108-04-9

English translation by H. G. Smittenaar copyright © 2006 Speck Press. Translated
from *De Cock en een variant op moord,* by Baantjer (Albert Cornelis Baantjer),
copyright © 1984 by Uitgeverij De Fontein bv, Baarn, Netherlands.

Library of Congress Cataloging-in-Publication Data
Baantjer, A. C.
[De Cock en een variant op moord. English]
DeKok and variations on murder : number twenty-one in the Inspector
DeKok series / Baantjer ; translated from the Dutch by H.G. Smittenaar.--
1st American ed.
p. cm.
ISBN-13: 978-1-933108-04-9 (pbk. : alk. paper)
ISBN-10: 1-933108-04-5 (pbk. : alk. paper)
1. DeKok, Inspector (Fictitious character)--Fiction. I. Smittenaar, H. G. II. Title.

PT5881.12.A2D5713 2006
839.31'364--dc22

2006007987

10 9 8 7 6 5 4 3 2 1

1

"Did you bury him?"

Archibald (Archie) Benson shook his head. He had a long, narrow face with sunken cheeks. A lock of black, greasy hair fell in front of his eyes. His hands shook as he lit his cigarette.

"I tried, but couldn't find a suitable spot."

The man in front of him grinned. Humorously.

"You're telling me the Kemner Dunes aren't large enough?" He cocked his head slightly as he gave the tall, slender figure of Archie a long, measured look. "Or did you get there and you forgot how to dig? It's child's play really, unless you never played in a sandbox as a kid."

Archie ignored the sarcasm.

"Look I said it was impossible. I'd have done it if I could have ... really!"

"So what did you do with the body?"

"Nothing."

The man's eyes flew open. He fixed his gaze on Benson, a look of disbelief on his face.

"Nothing?" he repeated steadily.

With a defeated shrug, Archie thumbed over his shoulder.

"He's still in the trunk."

The man stepped closer. He didn't stop until his face almost touched Archie's.

"Madman," he hissed. "We *have* to get rid of him. Do you not understand? Or, maybe, you'd like to spend the rest of your life in prison?"

Archie licked dry lips.

"Don't be ridiculous. Nobody wants to rot in jail."

The man leaned even closer.

"Get him out of here," he snarled.

For just a moment Archie Benson closed both eyes. The face so close in front of his own scared him. It was as if the eyes and the cruel mouth grew out of proportion. It was a face from a nightmare.

"I can't handle the job by myself," he said hesitantly. "Not on my own. The guy is huge. I tried twice to lift him out of the trunk. He's too damned heavy."

The man gave him a searing look.

"First you tell me you can't find the right place. Now one guy can't lift the corpse out of the trunk." There was suspicion in his voice.

Archie took a step backward, away from the face.

"I stopped at the edge of the sand dunes on the Sea Path, just outside Blomendaal. Some guys told me more than one corpse has been buried there."

The other man's look turned dangerous.

"You've been talking about our *job*?"

"No, I promise you. It's just something I heard … once."

The other nodded without conviction.

"In any event, you were on the Sea Path, near the dunes. What happened there?"

Archie swallowed nervously.

"As I struggled to lift the body out of the trunk, lights approached in the distance. As they came closer, I pushed the guy back into the trunk and closed it. The plan was to wait until the car passed me. But the cars kept on coming. After the third or fourth passed me I didn't feel like trying anymore."

"The cars kept coming?"

"I said so, didn't I? How was I to know there would be traffic that time of night."

The other slapped his forehead in frustration.

"My mistake was ever agreeing to work with you. It isn't as though nobody warned me."

He pushed his chin out.

"Where's the car now?"

"It's parked in the front."

"You have the keys?"

Archie felt in his pockets.

"What are you going to do?"

The other man snatched the keys out of Archie's hand. He grinned crookedly. His face set in a satanic grimace.

"Look at this as an opportunity for you to learn how to get rid of a corpse, and a bothersome witness ... permanently."

He turned on his heel and headed straight to the door.

Archibald Benson should have listened more carefully to the words of the other man. Maybe he was on overload or distracted. He followed the man outside obediently, head bowed. It was the last mistake he would make.

In Amsterdam, Detective Inspector DeKok of the Warmoes Street Police Station leaned back in his chair. He pulled his legs up, resting his heels on the edge of the desk. A groan of relief escaped him.

Vledder, his young partner, gave him a worried look. "Feet tired?"

The old man shook his head and smiled.

"I'm not in pain. My feet only get bad when an investigation goes sour, or I am getting nowhere. It is always a bad sign."

Vledder did not look convinced.

"Pain is pain. How many times has that happened?"

"How many times have my feet ached, or how many investigations have I bungled?"

"Investigations, of course."

DeKok did not answer at once. His broad, rugged face became pensive. For a moment Vledder thought his senior was ignoring him. DeKok was often lost in his thoughts.

"You know," he said after a long silence, "every investigator has his secrets carefully stowed away in the recesses of his brain. We know very well when we have failed. It's fortunate our failings seldom become public knowledge, otherwise our reputation would vanish on the wind." He fell silent again and pulled his lower lip out. He let it plop back. He repeated this annoying, unpleasant gesture several times.

"We're a lot like surgeons ... our mistakes get buried."

He shook his head, as if to clear it and then suddenly he grinned boyishly.

"By the way, do you know why surgeons wear rubber gloves?"

"To maintain the sterility of their procedures, I suppose," said Vledder, looking self-assured.

DeKok shook his head.

"They don't want to leave fingerprints at the scene of the crime."

"That's a terrible thing to say," smiled Vledder. "I'll be sure not to repeat it. We'll be accused of undermining the trust in the medical profession."

"Speaking of the medical profession, you know Dr. Eskes, don't you?"

"Of course, he's a toxicologist, one of our foremost forensic analysts."

"He is, indeed. Some time ago, one of our colleagues was called to a crime scene, where a young woman had died. Like most cops, he's as tenacious as a bulldog with a soup bone. Once he's decided on a theory he hates to let it go."

"Like you?"

"Never mind me. The young woman lived alone. One of her friends stopped by and accidentally found her dead. The friend summoned a doctor, but the doctor was too late to do anything but confirm the death."

"No coroner?"

"Not yet. Our colleague arrived. The first thing that struck him was the condition of the body. There wasn't a mark on it. The fact that the young woman had never complained about any physical illness or disability further aroused his suspicions. Absent any trauma or sign of struggle, our colleague thought of poison. Near the sink in the kitchen was an empty vial that had contained a prescription sleep remedy. On the kitchen table was a slice of meatloaf with one piece cut off and apparently eaten."

"The meatloaf was poisoned?"

"Unable to prove it, our colleague called Dr. Eskes. Eskes, however, felt the young woman had taken an overdose of sleeping tablets."

"Did he, at least, test the meatloaf?"

"That's what our colleague asked. But Dr. Eskes insisted it had nothing to do with the case. He said sleeping tablets don't work instantly and the woman might have felt like eating something."

"But, if she did eat some meatloaf, he should have tested it," said Vledder.

"Sure. Even though the sleeping tablets were in her system and had started to work, our colleague insisted the meatloaf could have been poisoned, as well."

"Very shrewd, I'd say."

"Yes, well, both Eskes and our colleague refused to change their positions. Finally our colleague demanded Dr. Eskes analyze the meal."

"And?"

"Dr. Eskes hesitated for just a moment. Then he took the remains of the slice of meatloaf and ate it."

"What?"

"Our colleague was dumfounded. He asked what Dr. Eskes thought he was doing. Eskes replied he was analyzing the meatloaf. 'If I'm dead tomorrow, it was poisoned,' he added."

"You can't be serious," said Vledder.

"No kidding. As you know the good doctor is alive and kicking."

Vledder grinned, but with the knowledge the detective in the story could have been him. Vledder, himself, had a tendency to settle on a theory. Once his mind was made up the facts had no bearing. Was DeKok giving him a subtle hint?

His musings were interrupted by the opening of the door to the detective room. The face of an old lady peeked around the door. When she saw the two men near the windows, she came farther into the room.

Vledder and DeKok looked at her, astonished. She was dressed in a flapper outfit, straight out of the twenties. She wore a small, cloche hat, complete with veil, and a short, black dress with fringe. She looked around shyly.

"May I come in?"

The inspectors nodded in unison. DeKok came from behind his desk and walked toward her. With a courtly little bow, he led her to the chair next to his desk.

"Please have a seat," he said in a cordial tone. "How may we be of service?"

She sat straight, a little stiff, in the chair. With a precise, practiced movement, she lifted her veil. She studied the faces before her.

"You're inspectors ... detectives?"

The old inspector gave her a winning smile.

"We have served in this capacity for years, many years, in my case. Please allow me to introduce myself: my name is DeKok, with, eh, with a kay-oh-kay." He waved in Vledder's direction. "And this is my partner, Dick Vledder."

The woman gave Vledder a searching look and turned back to DeKok.

"My name is Marlies, Marlies van Haesbergen. I must say ... this isn't easy. I have thought long and hard about what to do. Believe me, it took some sleepless nights before I dared come here."

DeKok looked at her with question in his eyes.

"Dared," he mused.

She nodded emphatically.

"It was not an easy decision. I fear you'll look on me as addled or foolish." She raised her sharp chin. Her eyes glistened with a mixture of bravado and apprehension. "I'm seventy-four years old, sometimes a bit eccentric and absent minded. However I am in no way demented or senile." She spoke in a firm tone, as if she was administering a lecture. "I trust you will take my story seriously. I hope you will believe me."

DeKok smiled uneasily.

"But we haven't any reason to … I mean, why would we not believe you?"

Her lips, surrounded by endearing wrinkles, pursed into an appealing pout.

"I'm well aware what people think of old people. If an elderly individual voices a suspicion, especially a vague suspicion, people dismiss it as a delusion."

"And that's what you came to do?"

Marlies van Haesbergen stared into the distance. The mistrust had gone from her eyes.

"I've come to the conclusion," she said softly, "that something terrible has happened to Mr. Vreeden."

DeKok was fascinated by the old woman. Her green, sparkling eyes kept him captivated. She must once have been a beauty. He leaned forward in a confidential manner.

"Who … eh, who is Mr. Vreeden?"

"You don't know?"

She moved in her chair.

"You should know who he is. Mr. Vreeden is an important man. He's the managing director of a multi-national corporation. His company conducts dredging operations all over the world."

"Dredging?"

Her eyes lit up.

"Holland is home to the world's foremost experts in dredging, water works, harbor building, dams, dikes, all of the above."

DeKok nodded vaguely. He searched his memory for any knowledge of dredging projects. Other than that massive, costly Delta Works storm-surge barrier project along Holland's southern coast and a small, asthmatic dredger in the Amsterdam canals, he couldn't think of any.

"So you believe something terrible has happened to the esteemed Mr. Vreeden?"

"Yes, I am convinced."

DeKok smiled.

"Why?"

"He's gone."

"Where did he go?"

Marlies van Haesbergen sighed.

"Nowhere ... he's dead."

DeKok felt he had to be careful. He must not show any signs of impatience.

"How do you know he's passed away?"

"He was dead in his chair."

"Where?"

She waved an arm in the direction of the windows.

"I found him in the company boardroom. It's also his office."

"When did you find him?"

"Four days ago."

DeKok and Vledder exchanged looks of amazement.

"Four days ago?" he exclaimed.

The old woman closed both eyes.

"I warned you about my vagueness—time doesn't have the meaning it once did." It sounded like an apology. "In any event I know how many sleepless nights I've passed."

DeKok relaxed.

"How did you happen to be in Mr. Vreeden's board-room?"

She nodded decisively, as if DeKok had finally come to the crux of it all.

"I live there. That is, in the building. The address is Emperors Canal 1217. My husband was the building custodian and concierge for nearly thirty years. We lived in an apartment on the top floor. When my husband died, Mr. Vreeden, himself, told me I could keep on living on the top floor."

She smiled, lost in memories. Then she continued.

"There's no custodian in the building anymore, nor is there a concierge. Mr. Vreeden modernized. An outside cleaning crew comes periodically, and there is a receptionist in the lobby. I still walk through the rooms in the building, before I go to bed. It is an old habit—helps me to feel everything is all right."

DeKok nodded his understanding.

"And during one of these nightly inspection tours, you found Mr. Vreeden?"

"Yes."

"Dead in his chair."

She hesitated for a moment.

"That's what I thought, yes."

DeKok rubbed his eyes.

"I have to tell you," he said in a tired voice, " I don't understand your hesitation."

Marlies van Haesbergen nodded encouragement.

"I understand perfectly. This is certainly my dilemma, as well. It is also why I've waited so long to tell you my story." She remained silent, as if gathering her thoughts. "Four days ago, during my inspection tour, as you call it,

I encountered Mr. Vreeden in his chair in the boardroom. It was startling, since he was never there that late. I managed to say something by way of greeting, but he did not answer. I took a few steps in his direction. He was leaning back, his eyes closed. In that moment there was no doubt he was dead."

"And then?"

"As soon as I could react I knew I must do something, phone someone."

"And did you?"

"No."

"Why not?"

She swallowed hard.

Once I picked up the phone in the boardroom, I realized it is connected to the switchboard. With no one there, I had to use the private line in my apartment."

"So you left the boardroom?"

She nodded, now looking fragile and weary.

"I took the elevator to go upstairs. But it's old and very slow. Meanwhile I wondered whom to call. Should I call a doctor, the police? Suddenly I realized, without examining him closely, I could not be sure he was dead. I hadn't even touched him to see whether he was cold."

"So you went back?"

Marlies wiped her forehead, her hand shaking.

"Yes, indeed, I returned. When I got off the elevator, I thought I heard something. Anxiously I went to the door of the boardroom. I was surprised to see the light was off because I recalled leaving the lights on." She pressed both hands to her eyes. "When I turned on the light, the chair was empty."

2

It took a while until Marlies van Haesbergen regained her composure. Her face was full of emotion. What little bravura she had shown in the beginning was gone. She now revealed herself as she probably was ... a dear, quiet, somewhat confused, old soul.

DeKok placed a reassuring hand on her shoulder. She was still shaking.

"The chair was empty?"

She released a deep sigh.

"Yes. He had utterly vanished. I couldn't believe my eyes—he had to be there. It occurred to me he might have slid off the chair, onto the floor. I went on my knees to look under the table. But nothing. Mr. Vreeden must have disappeared in the short time I rode the elevator up and down."

"How long would that have been?"

"It couldn't have been more than a few minutes."

For a long time DeKok stared at the wall, a pensive look on his face.

"Did it appear anything had been moved—the chair, it was in the same position as ... eh, before you left the room to go upstairs?"

She nodded several times.

"Everything looked exactly the same to me. Just Mr. Vreeden was no longer in the chair."

DeKok scratched the back of his neck.

"You said you thought you heard something as you stepped out of the elevator?"

"Yes."

"What exactly did you hear? What sort of sound?"

"It was a clicking sound."

"Like a lock?"

"Possibly. It was not very clear. Also my hearing isn't what it used to be."

DeKok ignored the remark.

"The front door was closed?"

Again she nodded vigorously. She seemed to have recovered. There was a fighting spirit in her eyes.

"I checked," she said firmly. "The front door was locked. Just like always. I also walked through the offices again and even looked into the restrooms. Nothing."

DeKok rubbed his chin.

"To whom have you told this story?"

She gave him a scornful look.

"I've spoken to no one, of course."

"Why not?"

Her eyes filled with disapproval at his lack of comprehension. She spread wide her hands.

"I may be old, but I'm not crazy. What in the world would I say?"

"You could tell them what you told me."

"Who would listen?"

"I am sure someone in the office would be worried about Mr. Vreeden's whereabouts."

Marlies van Haesbergen shook her head, disapproval on her face.

"The next morning," she said patiently, "I went to see

Mr. Vreeden's secretary. She seems a nice young woman, very attentive to his needs. She is very territorial about Mr. Vreeden, very protective. I asked to speak to Mr. Vreeden regarding my apartment. As excuses go it was a bit lame. She may have seen through me."

"And?"

"She said it would be out of the question for him to speak with me, for the next few days at least."

"What reason did she give?"

"Mr. Vreeden was out of the country on business."

DeKok narrowed his eyes.

"What else did she say?"

"She said, as soon as he came back, she would schedule a few minutes for me."

"What did you say?"

A sad smile played around her mouth.

"I agreed to wait until he came back. I said it wasn't all that urgent."

DeKok grinned.

"You should have told her Mr. Vreeden was dead, you had seen it yourself, and he wasn't ever going to come back."

Marlies pulled herself up straight and pressed her lips together in a disapproving frown. Her eyes spat fire.

"I do not know, Inspector, how you handle your own business," she said chiding him, "but life has taught me discretion. I'm an old woman. Worse still I am nobody, the widow of a concierge. Nobody every asked me to do my little inspection tours at night. They would see an old biddy who cannot keep her nose in her own business. In fact they would be within their rights to consider me a trespasser." She paused and took a deep breath. "Next you'll tell me you want me to report finding a corpse in the boardroom during one of these unauthorized tours. Oh, and tell them the corpse disappeared?" Her tone dripped with sarcasm and scorn. "Actually," she added, less vehemently, "there were moments I doubted the truth of what I'd seen with my own eyes. Was I confusing reality with a dream, an illusion?"

DeKok looked at her in a friendly way. He liked the way the old lady stood up for herself.

"In the end what led you to conclude," he asked gently, "something terrible did happen to Mr. Vreeden?"

She shook her head.

"It wasn't a conclusion based on fact. Except for my own observations in the boardroom, all I have is an uneasy feeling I've had since the incident. You could call it intuition."

"One more question. You have remained silent for four days. Why do you speak out now?"

"This afternoon, around the end of the business day, I returned to the office. I talked again to his secretary, asking her politely whether Mr. Vreeden had returned yet. She reacted out of character, distracted and annoyed. She said that there was no chance of seeing Mr. Vreeden for the foreseeable future."

"How did she explain that?"

"This time she said Mr. Vreeden was on holiday."

"What?"

Mrs. van Haesbergen nodded slowly.

"According to her he's now in the Bahamas."

Once the elderly lady left, the two partners fell silent. The strange story had made a deep impression upon DeKok.

He wondered whether he and Vledder could discover anything to explain the mysterious disappearance of Mr. Vreeden. This was, to put it mildly, a perplexing matter.

Vledder dragged a chair over to DeKok's desk. He sat on it backward, his arms across the back rest.

"Well, are you planning to pursue this?"

DeKok shrugged reluctantly.

"Marlies van Haesbergen is not the only one with a dilemma."

"How's that?"

DeKok rubbed the bridge of his nose with his little finger.

"Say we don't accept her story, we don't open an investigation. If Mr. Vreeden turns up dead, we are at fault for not doing so. If we pursue her supposition as a death and it turns out Mr. Vreeden is alive and well, we'll be the bumbling idiots who didn't know the difference between police business and a tale told by a senile, old woman."

Vledder nodded pensively.

"It sounds as though we take our chances, either way. Especially since this Mr. Vreeden seems to be a high-profile individual."

DeKok raised an admonishing finger in the air.

"Equally important, although the old lady's story is very intriguing, technically there's no evidence any law has been broken. A clear violation of the law is the standard for our interference."

Vledder looked surprised.

"Is one allowed to make someone disappear?"

DeKok shook his head.

"No, but the problem is one of semantics. The word

disappear does not appear in any of our law books. An unlawful act has to be defined there, as well as how it was executed and for what purpose." He paused and rubbed his chin, deep in thought. "That's the theory," he added as an after thought.

"What theory?"

"The theory in the law books concerning whether a crime has been committed," said DeKok curtly. "But the real problem here is one of credibility," he continued. "We have no evidence. On the one hand we have an elderly eccentric. On the other hand we have a conscientious secretary. One says Mr. Vreeden is dead. The other claims he's on vacation. I think we can accept the old lady's assertion regarding the secretary's behavior. Aside from the apparent contrast in the two women and their stories, was there a crime? If we focus on the disappearance, we're talking about the disappearance of a corpse."

"And that alone," grinned Vledder, "is sinister."

DeKok nodded slowly.

"It is," he agreed. "One question raises its ugly head: Why would anyone want to make the man's corpse disappear?"

Vledder gestured impatiently.

"They'd do it to cover up a crime, of course. What else?"

DeKok stared at his colleague.

"What crime? Even if Marlies van Haesbergen actually saw Mr. Vreeden dead in his office chair, his eyes were closed. He was quiet, apparently at peace. What she did not see is as important as what she did see. I mean, she said nothing to indicate Vreeden was the victim of violence. She saw no traumatic wounds, no weapons. What's more, the boardroom was undisturbed … both times she entered."

Vledder made another impatient gesture.

"Maybe she didn't look closely enough."

DeKok gave forth a short, scornful laugh.

"That is exactly my point. Did Marlies get a good look?" It sounded testy.

Vledder had no answer to that.

DeKok stood and started to pace up and down the detective room. It happened there were no other personnel present, so he could really stretch his legs. It helped him to order his thoughts. Perhaps, he thought, there's no crime at all. Perhaps Mr. Vreeden had just been taking a short nap after a long, tiring day. The executive chair in the board-room was probably very comfortable. Maybe he simply woke up after Marlies left. He could certainly have walked out of the building before she returned.

He grinned inwardly and chided himself silently. In his heart he knew nothing was ever that simple. He knew he was suppressing a feeling of foreboding. He began to see the arrival of the old lady at Warmoes Street as a harbinger. Would the mysterious events she related pull him into a tangle of nefarious activities? He felt he would need all his experience, perseverance, and intelligence in the days to come.

He looked at the wall clock in the detective room. It was almost ten o'clock. He took a few more turns up and down the room. Then he stopped next to Vledder.

"Where is that address that Marlies gave you?"

Vledder moved to his computer and touched a few keys. Then he took out his notebook and compared an entry in it with the screen.

"Eternal Lane," he said. "It is Eternal Lane, Number 752, Bergen."

The grey sleuth remained a moment longer in thought. Then he strode to the peg on the wall. He struggled into his raincoat and pushed his hat back on his head.

Vledder shut down his computer and joined DeKok.

"Where are we going?"

DeKok glanced over his shoulder.

"We're going to see who is at home in Bergen."

Vledder had a look of consternation on his face.

"What if we do find Vreeden at home?"

DeKok grinned broadly.

"Then I'll shake the hand of a man who has risen, like Lazarus, from the dead."

Vledder stared.

"Is that a joke?"

"No, I'm deadly serious."

"You mean—"

DeKok interrupted.

"I'm convinced our Mr. Vreeden is no longer among the living."

3

Vledder maneuvered the old police car, a VW Beetle, skillfully through heavy traffic in the inner city.

It started to rain. Holland has one of the highest rainfall averages in the world. Combined with Holland's elevation, mostly below sea level, heavy rainfall creates some interesting, temporary traffic conditions. Hollanders routinely defy the odds their country will end up underwater. Vigilance and superb engineering have reduced the odds of a catastrophic flood in the Netherlands to a one in 10,000 year event.

The car progressed to the outskirts of the city. DeKok found himself transfixed by the reflections of neon signs on the slick pavement. They were almost as brilliant as a low-lying sun. With effort he tore his eyes away from the road and the lull of the window wipers. As he refocused his eyes, the car passed an experimental development. Houses, buildings, and streets floated on caissons in a large lake. The structures were securely anchored to strong, vertical, concrete-and-steel poles. If the water rose, the entire development would rise with it, remaining in place relative to its surroundings. It was a model of Dutch innovation, one answer to catastrophic flooding.

DeKok was not sure he approved. He trusted the ancient system of dikes. They dated back to the sixteenth century. Windmills supported the system, continuously pumping water out of the low lands into the sea. Now there was continual talk of global warming. If the polar icecaps were to melt, tiny Holland would disappear completely under the water. DeKok, as all of his countrymen, knew the sea had a head start.

His thoughts turned away from thoughts of cataclysmic flooding. For generations the Dutch had lived their lives, in spite of the omnipresent threat.

With a sigh he sank lower in the seat, a stubborn expression on his face.

Vledder glanced at him.

"I'm still trying to figure out your motives," he said at last. "You want to go to Bergen to see if Vreeden is at home. In almost the same breath you tell me that you think he's dead."

DeKok opened his eyes. He had started to doze.

"An opinion," he said slowly, "is not the same as knowledge. I can't act on intuition. At best it spurs me on to find out more. But if I'm to get involved and call this a case, I'll have to prove Vreeden is no longer alive."

"How?"

DeKok grinned sadly.

"For one thing, I need his corpse."

"And you expect to find it in his villa in Bergen?"

DeKok pursed his lips.

"I don't think that's likely."

"So, where would you start to look?"

The old inspector sighed.

"If the man hasn't been home for four days," he said patiently, "we'll find traces. There will be unopened mail, unread newspapers, that sort of thing. I hope to find some support for my opinion, my surmise." He pushed himself up in the seat. "Of course," he went on, "the easiest thing would be to ask his secretary his exact whereabouts."

Vledder nodded in agreement.

"Frankly, I thought visiting his office would be your first move."

DeKok shook his head.

"I don't think it would be wise. I would have to explain to his secretary why I'm interested in Mr. Vreeden."

"His suspected death isn't enough?"

"No, his secretary would just give me a lovely smile and tell me Mr. Vreeden is in the Bahamas on holiday."

Vledder took one hand off the wheel and waved it nonchalantly.

"Then we'll go to the Bahamas to verify it."

DeKok laughed out loud.

"I think that our esteemed commissaris would have a heart attack. The expense alone would send him into a fit." He had to stop himself from enjoying the image. "In any event, it's not that simple," he continued. "To involve us officially I must have evidence to point to Vreeden's murder. We must have judicial standing to get the commissaris' approval to act. Sharing Marlies van Haesbergen's story won't get us anywhere. I also wonder if I'm allowed to do that."

"Do what?"

"Share the story with any official."

"I don't see the harm?"

DeKok shook his head, as if to clear it.

"If Vreeden is really dead, somebody is responsible. Marlies is the only witness. Sharing her confidence could put her in harm's way. Her own subconscious fear could explain why she waited four days before coming to the police."

They drove on in silence for awhile.

When they left the city behind, the rain intensified. Vledder increased the speed of the wipers, and DeKok sank back down in the seat. He pushed his dilapidated felt hat down over his eyes. Vledder concentrated on the road, but there was a thoughtful look on his face.

"If we can't release the story and can't act in any official capacity," said Vledder, breaking the silence, "it seems ridiculous to look into it. Maybe we're just snooping. Perhaps we should bide our time, until someone comes forward to report Mr. Vreeden missing."

DeKok pushed his head back.

"And who would that be? Vreeden isn't married, has no children, and appears to have no close friends. It could take a long, long time for anybody to realize he's disappeared."

Vledder did not answer at once, but his face mirrored his dissatisfaction with the answer.

After a while he ventured, "You've pretty much convinced me the man is dead. If his secretary maintains he's on vacation in the Bahamas, she must be involved with his death."

DeKok pushed himself up in the seat and peered over the dashboard.

"She could well be," he said, scanning the surroundings, "but it doesn't have to be that way. She could have been misled by someone in authority or, at least, someone she would believe."

Vledder shook his head in irritation.

"DeKok, this is a mess!"

DeKok laughed.

"Watch it, Dick," he said. "We have to make a left turn here to get to Bergen."

Like Seaside, Bergen is primarily a vacation resort. The whipping rain had cleaned the streets and it had driven the holiday makers indoors. *Bello*, a, legendary steam locomotive, was the central town monument. Usually the center of holiday activity, it stood deserted and forlorn.

The sight of *Bello* reminded DeKok of an earlier visit to the coast, a few years before. He'd been sent there because of the dramatic death of a nurse, Georgette Mirabeau. As he recalled it was about the same time of the year.

Even now DeKok wondered what could they hope to accomplish?

They left the town center, driving in the direction of Schoorl. Eternity Lane was a narrow, twisting road, flanked by impressive elm trees. From the road they saw luxurious villas and bungalows, half-hidden by luscious greenery. The house numbers were all but invisible under landscaping, and it was too dangerous to park on the narrow road. Vledder entered a driveway, got out of the car, and examined the number on the gate post. It was number 748. He got behind the wheel, backed out, and entered another driveway two houses down.

Mr. Vreeden's house was a lavish villa in a style reminiscent of the 1930s. It was a stately, elegant home, embellished by painted wooden trim and protruding, sculpted gutters. The place appeared deserted, no lighted windows.

To get the car off the road Vledder drove to the back of the house. The partners left the car and walked down a narrow, paved alley to the imposing front door. They stopped under the portico.

Vledder looked at DeKok.

"Do we ring the bell?"

DeKok nodded.

"It's the usual thing when you visit someone."

Vledder hesitated.

"What do we say if someone answers the door bell?"

"I don't know yet," shrugged DeKok. "I'm sure I'll think of something."

There was a discreet brass push button in the white lacquered door jam. Vledder pressed the button. They heard chimes echo through the house. The sound died away and the seconds ticked by.

Nothing happened.

Vledder pressed the bell for the second time.

"It looks as though," he said nervously, "nobody is home."

They waited an obligatory several minutes before walking around the building. The garden was in bloom and well maintained. The paths were inviting and uncluttered, surrounded by white and red rhododendrons. The heavy aroma of flowers penetrated the rain.

When they returned to the front door, DeKok took a small, brass cylinder from his pocket. It was his "magic door opener," made for him by a master ex-burglar. DeKok had never found a lock he could not open with the ingenious device.

Vledder looked worried.

"We don't have a warrant, you know."

DeKok merely smiled. He expertly selected a combination, glanced again at the lock, made a small adjustment, and inserted the instrument into the keyhole. Within seconds there was a soft click and the heavy door opened soundlessly. Both inspectors entered.

The beam of his flashlight danced through the spacious lobby, resting for a moment on a beautiful grandfather clock. The clock stood against skillfully carved oaken wainscoting. DeKok approved.

"The wainscoting is all original," he murmured appreciatively.

Vledder did not respond. He felt uneasy. In sharp contrast to DeKok's apparently cavalier attitude, he could not reconcile himself with illegally entering any building, let alone someone's home. This wouldn't be the first time he silently cursed "Handie" Henkie. Henkie and DeKok had been on opposite sides of the law as younger men. Each was meticulous in his methods and each bore the other a begrudging admiration. Sometime after his "retirement," Henkie gave DeKok his lock-picking tool. Still, as frustrating as DeKok could be, Vledder never wavered in his loyalty and regard for his senior.

"One of these days we'll get into trouble because of that burglar's tool," he whispered.

As ever, DeKok ignored the remark.

"Take a look in the mailbox," he said.

Like most houses of its era, this one had a brass-lined mail slot in the door. On the inside of the door a box with a small door caught the mail. Vledder checked the mailbox, but reported it empty.

"Not a single thing here," he emphasized. "There isn't even any dust."

To the right of the foyer, DeKok carefully opened a door. It revealed a large, rectangular room with an enormous desk as its centerpiece. The inspector approached the desk and played his flashlight over the top. It was almost too in order. A row of pens was perfectly aligned at the top of a large blotter, and a desktop calendar showed the correct date.

DeKok circled the desk and sat down in the majestic swivel chair. He pulled on a couple of drawers. They were not locked. His fingers brushed through papers, making a dry, rustling sound. The contents of the drawers were, primarily, drawings of various harbor installations. There were also business letters on dredging company letterhead.

Vledder came to stand next to him. He shook his head in disapproval.

"Tell me you did not just add illegal search and seizure to breaking in," he said. "Besides the legal implications, Inspector, it's not ... decent."

DeKok gave him a sharp look.

"To do away with a man or a corpse is against the law and, I'm sure you agree, indecent."

He returned his attention to the desk and studied the contents of the drawers. Suddenly a thin booklet with a dark blue cover caught his eye. He took it out of the drawer and placed it on the blotter. His fingers shook slightly as he opened the booklet. Vledder leaned over for a closer look.

"A passport," he whispered.

DeKok nodded agreement.

"It's a valid passport, issued in Paul Vreeden's name."

Vledder swallowed hard. "He could not have gone on vacation in the Bahamas without a passport."

DeKok did not respond. He looked at the photograph. The man's face was angular, with a broad, strong chin. A man, he mused, with the exterior of someone who knows exactly what he wants.

"Length: one meter eighty-five," he read aloud. "Color of eyes: grey-green." He barked his short, scornful laugh. "At least we know what to look for in a corpse."

Vledder crouched down next to the desk and picked up the passport. While DeKok held the flashlight beam on the booklet, Vledder turned the pages in the back.

"Well," said Vledder, "our Mr. Vreeden is a real globetrotter." There was a reluctant admiration in his voice. "He's been to more than vacation spots—traveled a good deal in the Near East. He's been to all the OPEC countries, Iran, Iraq, Kuwait, Yemen, Saudi Arabia." He pushed the passport back at DeKok. "Apparently he's had regular contacts there ... either that or he really likes the food."

"Is this history or current events?"

"What do you mean?"

"When did he make these trips?"

"Almost all of them were this year."

DeKok took the passport from Vledder and weighed it in his hand. With a resolute gesture he placed it in his inside coat pocket. He then fished a large, silken handkerchief from another pocket. He carefully wiped all the surfaces on the desk and the drawers he had touched.

"A good burglar," he grinned, "doesn't leave fingerprints."

Suddenly he froze. There was a noise outside. He jumped out of the seat and walked quickly toward the foyer.

Vledder followed.

The front door opened. A hand felt for the light switch. The light revealed a neatly dressed man. The man's eyes were wide with astonishment as he surveyed the two smiling detectives who flanked the grandfather clock in the foyer.

Still smiling, DeKok took a step forward and bowed lightly.

"I don't think I have had the pleasure," he purred. "Who might you be?"

The man suppressed his amazement with apparent difficulty.

"Johan," he said. "I'm Johan, Mr. Vreeden's butler."

4

It took a while before Johan gained a full grasp of the situation. His bewilderment quickly turned to an expression of arrogant deference. His handsome face had the look of the maitre d' in an exclusive restaurant forced to seat two men wearing shirtsleeves and no ties. He closed his mouth and frowned slightly. He looked up and down DeKok's figure with ill concealed disdain.

"Who are you?"

It was a demand, not a question.

DeKok's smile froze on his face. His eyes had a cold, hard look.

"My name," he said amiably, "is DeKok, with a kay-oh-kay." He pointed in Vledder's direction. "And this is my colleague, Vledder. We're police officers."

"Inspectors?"

DeKok nodded.

"We're attached to Warmoes Street Station in Amsterdam."

The butler leaned his head farther back, as if trying to view the inspectors from a greater height.

"May I ask how you gained entrance?"

DeKok made an apologetic gesture.

"The door was open," he lied.

Johan shook his head.

"That's quite impossible," he blustered. "When I left, I locked the door. It is my job to see after such things."

"It was open," insisted DeKok. "We were surprised as well." He carefully studied the butler's face. "The fact is, we were … *are* worried. Otherwise we would not have entered, open door or not."

"The police are worried?"

DeKok nodded emphatically.

"Mr. Vreeden sounded apprehensive, when he tele-phoned and asked me to come to his house."

Johan frowned.

"Mr. Vreeden called you?" he asked, disbelief in his voice. "He asked you to come here?"

DeKok spread both hands, palms out.

"He said that he had some serious difficulties, or expected some trouble, in his Amsterdam office."

"What sort of trouble?"

DeKok laughed sheepishly. His weather-beaten face looked innocent, a bit stupid. On the inside he enjoyed himself hugely. Sometimes the game was just good fun.

"That's what he was going to tell us. He offered to meet in person. I tried to get some idea what it was all about, but he seemed hesitant to discuss details over the phone."

"What time did he call you?"

DeKok asked Vledder what time it was. Vledder told him.

"It must have been about an hour, an hour and a half ago. We came straight here after the phone call."

Butler Johan did not answer at once. He took his time, restoring his supercilious attitude. He divested himself of his coat in slow movements, hanging it on the coat rack in the foyer. Then he walked closer to DeKok.

"I'm afraid," he said insolently, "you have been the victim of a bad joke. Mr. Vreeden could not have called you for an appointment. He is not in the Netherlands. Mr. Vreeden has been in the Bahamas for several days." He paused. "I would have certainly heard about any difficulties in the office. Messrs. Grauw and Middelkoop would surely have informed me, so there have been none."

DeKok had a questioning look.

"And who are these Messrs. Grauw and Middelkoop?"

"They are company co-directors."

The old sleuth nodded his understanding.

"May I use your telephone to call either or both of the gentlemen? You see the phone call we received sounded authentic."

The butler's face went red.

"No, you may *not* have permission to use the telephone. Trust me. There are no difficulties in the office. You may also dismiss the notion it was Mr. Vreeden who called you. May I reiterate? I personally assisted Mr. Vreeden with his preparations. I, myself, drove Mr. Vreeden to Schiphol for his flight to the Bahamas, and saw him off."

DeKok rubbed his chin in a gesture of bafflement.

"You are certain his travel documents were all in order?"

Johan nodded.

"Of course. Again, it is my job to ensure everything is in order for my employer's trips. I check his luggage, travel documents, ticketing."

DeKok looked up. Suddenly the vague expression melted, and the butler was confronted by a hard, sardonic face.

"Ah yes, the ticketing was all arranged," DeKok said slowly. A hard grin, devoid of joy, played around his lips. "But

Mr. Vreeden's tickets, rather his ticket, was one-way. He may have gone to heaven, or he may have gone to hell. But you're esteemed employer's destination was *not* the Bahamas."

The return to Amsterdam was more leisurely. The rain had stopped and the night sky was clear with bright twinkling stars and a pale half-moon.

DeKok looked out of the windshield, but the beauty of the sky could not lift his somber mood. He regretted having had to use lies to explain his presence in the villa. He reflected, ruefully, he'd do it again if the situation demanded. He felt for Vreeden's passport inside his pocket. It was a trump card, but one he realized he would not be able to use. He'd come by it illegally. Dick Vledder was right in calling his method of acquiring it unreasonable search and seizure. He had clearly exceeded his authority.

"Our authority is so restricted," he said suddenly out loud, "our hands are, more often than not, tied."

Vledder looked askance.

"It's about time you abide by those restrictions. The arrival of that butler put us squarely behind the eight ball."

"Ach," said DeKok. "He'll just have to swallow the story of the open door."

"But was it wise?"

"What?"

"Was it wise to let the guy know you think Vreeden is dead?"

DeKok shrugged.

"I don't know what's wise or unwise in this instance," he answered, irked. "I've seldom felt as stupid as this. It's like running around with a blindfold in a dark room."

Vledder laughed.

"Leaves you in the dark, but it could be worse."

"Oh, yes?"

"Yes, you could be searching an unlighted cellar at midnight for a black cat that isn't there."

DeKok smiled. Then his face became serious again.

"Trouble is," he said, "we're fumbling around because this is so vague. I *am* certain of one thing, however, the butler is lying."

"He was most unpleasant, but how can we prove he lied?"

"There you put your finger on it. The whole thing comes down to the same thing. We need evidence. We need evidence to show that Vreeden is dead."

Vledder sighed in sympathy.

"Perhaps," he offered, "we can contact the authorities in the Bahamas, and ask them to, at least, verify his whereabouts."

DeKok shook his head.

"You'll remember that the butler told us Vreeden did not leave a forwarding address."

"Isn't that strange in and of itself?"

DeKok shook his head vigorously.

"For someone in Mr. Vreeden's position it is more than strange. His voice became theatrical. "Any director of such a large, multi-national corporation would be available to someone, even while vacationing. He has too much at stake." He paused and made a soothing gesture. "But it is possible for a fatigued or spent executive to suddenly decide he's had enough and sever all contact and take a leave of absence."

"In that case we could send his description to the Bahamas."

DeKok grinned.

"The Bahamas, my dear boy, consists of more than three thousand islands, riffs, and capes, spread out over more than a thousand miles."

Vledder was dumbfounded.

"I never knew you had a penchant for geography."

DeKok shook his head.

"I don't," he said tiredly. "Before your time I had to deal with a perpetrator who fled from Amsterdam to the Bahamas. I called the police in their capital, Nassau. Nassau is on the island of New Providence. I asked if they could look out for him. They laughed at me and explained the logistical nightmare they would face. I was sufficiently ashamed of my ignorance to look at an atlas."

"Well, that means we can forget the police there."

DeKok chewed on his lower lip.

"If everybody insists Vreeden is somewhere in the Bahamas, we'll have a hard time proving he isn't."

Vledder reacted with irritation.

"We can't just let it go at that, surely?"

DeKok gave him a glance that spoke volumes.

"Why not? One of these days somebody besides us is going to wonder about Mr. Vreeden." He pressed himself upright in the seat and looked outside. "We're back in town," he said with a relived tone of voice.

Vledder nodded.

"You want me to drop you off at home?"

"What time is it?"

Vledder looked deliberately at the clock on the dashboard. DeKok had a wristwatch, but he never consulted it. It was too modern for his taste. He often talked sentimentally about the watch he had inherited from his grandfather, an enormous stainless steel thing with a long chain, designed to be kept in a vest pocket.

"A little after twelve thirty," he said. "In the morning," he added superfluously.

"Just go on to the station house," decided DeKok. "We'll park the car and have a nightcap at Little Lowee's."

Lowee's birth name was Louis. Because of his diminutive size, he was invariably called "Little Lowee." For years he had owned and managed the dim, intimate space near the corner of Barn Alley. With a certain amount of pride, he referred to it as "my establishment." But to most of the underworld it was always known as "Little Lowee's place." It was also a favorite haunt of DeKok.

The small barkeep greeted DeKok enthusiastically. He shook him by the hand. His mousy face was transformed by a broad, welcoming smile. Lowee was one of DeKok's greatest admirers. He genuinely liked the old inspector. DeKok liked Lowee as well, but he wasn't above taking advantage of their friendship, if need be. Some might term DeKok's exploitation of the small bartender shameless. But Lowee never seemed to mind. Vledder knew DeKok and Lowee went way back, predating his time on the force. He also knew the friendship was not one-sided. DeKok protected his small friend as often as he asked him for information or for help on a case.

"The later the hour, the more welcome the guests," chirped Lowee in flawless Dutch. Then he continued in his more usual gutter language. "But I gotta say, DeKok, I ain't bin expectin' you guys dis late."

Lowee spoke a kind of Dutch called bargeons that most

Dutchmen would be hard put to recognize. It was the language of his world, of these streets. Although DeKok spoke and understood the vernacular perfectly, he seldom used it.

He smiled benignly at his friend as he hoisted himself on a stool at the end of the bar, his back against the wall. He knew very well that Lowee had broken just about every law of God or man at one time or another, but he did not judge. On the contrary, in his own way, DeKok loved the little crook.

"I was afraid," he said, as he settled himself, "you'd loose sleep if I didn't show up."

Lowee grinned.

"Same recipe?"

Without waiting for an answer, he dove under the bar and produced a venerable bottle of cognac. He briefly held it up for DeKok to see and then placed three snifters on the bar. With skillful movements he removed the cork and poured three generous portions into the glasses.

"Busy?" asked Lowee as he placed the bottle on the counter.

DeKok shrugged.

"One thing we never have … a slump in crime," he said. It was one of his stock answers.

He leaned forward, lifted the glass, warmed it in his hand, and took a sip. With eyes closed he let the golden liquid trickle down his throat.

Now Lowee and Vledder also lifted their glasses and silently savored the first few sips.

Then Little Lowee leaned over the bar.

"If you hadna come," he whispered hoarsely, "I woulda come by da coop temorro."

DeKok laughed.

"What coop?" he asked.

"Da Warmoes coop, da copcoop."

"Why a coop?"

"Well, you knows, you guys sit there waitin' for some crook to lay an egg. Den you runs aroun' like chickens widout heads. Chicken coop, cop coop. Gedit?"

DeKok laughed heartily. Vledder smiled sourly.

"I like it," said DeKok. "Rings true. But I don't see you volunteering to visit!"

"Nossir, it ain't a primo tourist attraction."

"So, what did you need me for?"

"I godda to talk at you."

DeKok noted the suddenly serious face on the other side of the bar.

"Problems?"

"Not me."

"Well, go on ..."

Lowee stole a glance around the room to make sure nobody was listening. The only other customers were prostitutes, through for the evening. They talked animatedly among themselves, paying no attention to the group at the bar. Doubtless they would have recognized DeKok and Vledder as police officers. They would immediately dismiss them as prospective customers. In addition the police seldom bothered members of the oldest profession. It was, after all, a legitimate business in Holland.

When Lowee had satisfied himself he leaned closer again.

"Ya know Black Archie?"

"Archie Benson—isn't he Fat Nellie's son?"

"He's da one," nodded Lowee.

"Go on," urged DeKok.

"Well I'm sorta worried about da guy. He usta come inna place alla time. For four days he ain't showed. Ain't bin home—I axed. Archie, he's a regular guy, but not too smart. You gotta know he's in deep, eh, trouble."

DeKok gave Lowee a long look.

"Since when did you get the degree in social work?"

Lowee shrugged.

"Fat Nellie is some kinda relative to me. She did wanna come n' see ya, but she's sort shy. She wants me ta talk to you."

DeKok placed his empty glass on the bar.

"What's the matter with the boy?"

Lowee sighed elaborately.

"Search me. Coupla days ago he was playin' cards with some guys. Sudden like he says, 'Where can you bury a body?' One of them guys wanna be funny and says, 'Inna Simmetry.' Well, Archie got mad and throwed is cards onna table. Then he says, 'Idiot, it ain't *that* kinda body.' Well I ask you, DeKok, don't that sound like trouble?"

5

DeKok got off the streetcar at Station Square. From there he ambled across the Damrak. He enjoyed the view, especially on a sunny day like today. The wide gateway to Amsterdam was colorful and inviting. There were flags around the docks for the sightseeing boats. They waved against a clear blue sky. The façade of the Stock Exchange building had recently been cleaned and looked like white marble. The terraces of the many bars and restaurants filled with tourists, descending like a flock of birds.

DeKok was in a good mood. A brief, intense, sleep had recharged his batteries. He loved listening to the various languages people spoke in these gathering places. He watched the families lining up to take the tour on Amsterdam's canals. He glanced appreciatively at beautiful, young women in abbreviated summer dresses.

He'd left the world of crime for a brief respite. It lay slumbering in a strange, faraway land. For the moment it didn't concern him.

He should have turned off to reach Warmoes Street at Old Bridge Alley. But his elation at being free drove him on to Dam Square. He found an inviting bench, sat down, and watched the pigeons. A tall, skinny man crouched down and fed the pigeons from his hands. The birds fluttered around him, some roosting on his head. Each waited for a turn at the food. DeKok drank in the charming tableau to the fullest.

Suddenly, behind the man and the pigeons, DeKok sighted an old lady crossing the square. She came from the direction of New Church and walked in the direction of Kalver Street, the foremost shopping street in all of Holland. DeKok was less interested in her posture and bearing than in her attire. She wore a little round hat with a veil and a short, narrowly cut dress in the flapper style.

"Marlies," he whispered to himself. "Marlies van Haesbergen."

He stood up, walked around the man with the pigeons and began to follow the woman. His body reacted without input from his brain. Intuition compelled him to follow where she led.

Kalver Street was crowded, despite the early hour. But he had no trouble keeping Marlies in sight. The little round hat bobbed up and down like a buoy in the sea of people.

All at once, however, he had lost her. The little hat had disappeared. DeKok cursed himself. He stopped and looked around. With a sigh of relief he rediscovered her in front of a perfumery. He stood across the street, careful his reflection couldn't be observed in the window on the opposite side.

Apparently something had attracted her because she entered the shop. A few minutes later she emerged with a small parcel in a plastic bag. After a last glance at the window, she continued down Kalver Street.

The Mint Tower was already in sight when she turned right, down Holy Way. There, too, she seemed to be interested in shop windows. DeKok stayed out of her field of vision with some difficulty. Just as DeKok convinced himself Marlies was merely on a shopping trip, she entered a travel agency.

DeKok waited patiently. Marlies took her time. It was at least twenty minutes before she emerged. She retraced her steps down Holy Way to Kalver Street.

The old inspector hesitated for a moment. Then he crossed the street and entered the travel agency.

A handsome woman, around forty, reached her side of the counter at about the same time DeKok reached his.

"How may I help you?" asked the woman.

DeKok produced his most winning smile.

"I'd like to ask you what the elderly client, who just left, was doing here."

The woman looked at him for several seconds, a surprised look on her face.

Her tone was curt and disapproving. "That's none of your business," she said.

DeKok nodded his understanding.

"It *is* my business," he said firmly, but amiably. "I'm a police inspector, assigned to Warmoes Street Station." He felt in an inside pocket for his identification. "It is of the utmost importance to know why Mrs. van Haesbergen came here."

"You know her?"

DeKok pursed his lips.

"I've met her," he said.

The woman turned around and walked to an impeccably dressed gentleman in a gray flannel suit, seated at a desk. After some whispering they returned to the counter together. The gentleman inspected DeKok's identification at length. Then he wrote the inspector's name on a note pad.

"Make sure you watch the 'kay-oh-kay.' I'm rather proud of that," said DeKok.

The man behind the counter gave him an irritated look.

"If you know Mrs. van Haesbergen, why don't you ask her why she was here?"

"I fear she won't tell me the truth."

The impeccable gentleman sighed dramatically.

"Mrs. van Haesbergen," he said finally, "booked a trip with us."

DeKok nodded patiently.

"Her destination?"

"Georgetown, Great Exuma."

DeKok narrowed his eyes. He was not pleased having to extract answers.

"And Great Exuma is where?" he prompted.

The man looked surprised at DeKok's apparent ignorance.

"Sir, it is in the Bahamas."

DeKok opened the door of the crowded detective room. He ambled toward Vledder in his typical, duck-footed gait. Vledder was busily typing away on his computer keyboard.

"Has Little Lowee any idea the identity of the body?" he asked.

Vledder rested his fingers and looked up.

"No, he called about half an hour ago. He told me he had done his best, but he had no new news." Vledder grinned. "I'm sure that was the gist of his report. Over the telephone his Bargoens sounds even more like gibberish than it does in person. Anyway," he added spitefully, "it seems the underworld isn't omniscient, after all."

DeKok ignored the latter comment.

"We can hang on for a while. Lowee hasn't had a lot of time to ask his contacts," he said as he sailed his dilapidated little hat in the direction of the peg on the wall and missed. He left the hat on the floor and sat down behind his desk.

"What do we know about Archie?"

Vledder made a few entries on his keyboard and then pushed it away.

"Lowee says there's still no sign of him." He paused and looked pensively at DeKok.

"Where have you been this morning?"

DeKok rubbed the bridge of his nose with his little finger.

"I followed a woman."

"You what?"

"Yes."

"At your age?" he teased.

"What about my age?" queried DeKok.

Vledder shrugged.

"A bit old to be pursuing women, I'd say."

DeKok mumbled something uncomplimentary.

"One is never too old," he answered, irked. "But I wasn't following just any woman and it certainly wasn't romantic. I saw Marlies van Haesbergen on Dam Square and I decided to follow her. This morning she booked a trip to the Bahamas."

Vledder was genuinely surprised this time.

"What?"

DeKok nodded calmly.

"She appears to be headed for Georgetown on Great Exuma."

"How do you know?"

"I saw her enter a travel agency. I waited till she left. Then I went in and asked what she had been doing there."

Vledder shook his head in bewilderment.

"What business does she have in the Bahamas?"

Commissaris Buitendam, the tall, stately police chief of Warmoes Street Station, waved with a narrow, elegant hand, "Have a seat, DeKok."

"I'd rather stand," DeKok reacted, stubbornly. There was no personal enmity between DeKok and his commissaris. His aversion to these meetings was based on the latter's tendency to limit his, DeKok's, authority and freedom of movement. DeKok clung to his own opinions and trusted his own methods when it came to detective work.

Buitendam made an appeasing gesture.

"As you like." He paused to make an impression, stretched his back in the chair and took a deep breath. "I'm afraid you have gone too far this time, DeKok. Our judge advocate, Mr. Schaap, has just called me and he takes your actions very seriously."

DeKok feigned surprise.

"What actions?"

The commissaris cleared his throat.

Mr. Meturovski, an attorney for Dredging Works Vreeden, has filed a complaint against you and Vledder."

"What is the nature of this complaint?"

Commissaris Buitendam brought both hands together, forming a steeple. It was a gesture of superiority.

"He accuses you of illegal entry and trespassing."

"What?"

The commissaris frowned.

"Was I not clear enough?"

DeKok nodded.

"Certainly, I understood what you said. But the complaint astounds me—it is completely unjustified. Neither Vledder nor I would gain illegal entry, nor would we trespass."

Buitendam consulted his notes.

"The complaint states you and Vledder illegally entered the domicile of a Mr. Vreeden last night. This is the testimony of a Mr. Johan Mindere, butler on the Bergen premises, who surprised you and Vledder in the foyer of his employer's home."

"That's correct."

The commissaris grinned supremely.

"So, it *was* trespass and illegal entry."

DeKok shook his head.

"I object to the characterization of our presence there as illegal. Circumstances dictated we enter the villa."

"Please explain yourself."

DeKok made a tired gesture.

"Last night," he lied with conviction, "I received a telephone call from a man who represented himself as Mr. Vreeden. He told me he was the managing director of a large dredging outfit, located at Emperor's Canal." He looked into the commissarial eyes. "And that's well inside our precinct."

The commissaris nodded agreement.

"Mr. Vreeden," continued DeKok, "said that he had discovered some serious problems in his office. He asked to see me, personally."

"What sort of problems?"

DeKok spread both hands in a gesture of helplessness.

"That, I don't know. Naturally I asked him. He was reluctant to elaborate, other than to say he suspected criminal activities. As he refused to discuss it further over the telephone, I invited him to visit us at the station."

"And?"

"Mr. Vreeden said it was impossible for him to come to Amsterdam. He was in his house in Bergen, unwilling to leave. His exact words were, 'I am afraid to leave the house.'"

"And he did not tell you why?"

DeKok shook his head, a regretful look on his face.

"No, Commissaris." The old sleuth released a deep sigh. "Although his remarks were a bit vague, I became alarmed enough to immediately drive to Bergen. Vledder drove, of course."

The commissaris nodded with a faint smile. He knew all about DeKok's driving abilities.

"Go on," he urged.

"When we arrived at the villa, it appeared strangely deserted. There were no lights visible anywhere. This, in addition to the fact we found the front door unlocked, aroused our suspicions. We felt obliged to investigate further." He smiled apologetically. "We had barely closed the door behind us when the butler showed up."

Commissaris Buitendam frowned as he looked for several seconds at his old, experienced subordinate. Then two red spots appeared on his cheeks.

"DeKok," he said in a shaking voice, "that story is a lie from beginning to end."

DeKok shrugged.

"My old mother always said, 'Child, I cannot make you *believe* anything.' She meant she could not give me faith. But the principle is the same, I think."

The commissaris was becoming angrier by the moment.

"I'm not remotely interested in what your mother said, or meant."

DeKok looked innocent.

Buitendam swallowed in an obvious attempt to regain some sense of control. His Adams' apple whipped up and down. It took some time for him to regain some composure.

"Listen, DeKok," he said finally, trying to be reasonable, "Mr. Vreeden is on vacation in the Bahamas as we speak. Therefore your story is more than farfetched, it is ludicrous. Next, the butler swears under oath that he had locked the front door himself. To make matters worse Messrs. Grauw and Middelkoop, Mr. Vreeden's co-directors, testified. They deny difficulties of any sort at the offices of the company at Emperor's Canal, let alone criminal misdeeds."

DeKok grinned broadly.

"In that case, why would I go to Bergen?"

Commissaris Buitendam's reaction was unusually sharp.

"That is precisely why I am demanding an explanation."

DeKok pushed his chin forward. There was a pugnacious expression on his face. Fire burned in the back of his eyes.

"You don't seriously expect me," he said cynically, "to acquiesce to false accusations against me and my partner." He shook his head. "You can forget self-incrimination. I will gladly offer a full explanation of my actions in answer to a complaint signed and delivered by Mr. Vreeden in person. You can tell *that* to the judge advocate."

Commissaris Buitendam stood up behind his desk.

He was crimson, down to his chest. His nostrils quivered. Shaking with anger he pointed at the door.

"OUT!" he screamed.

DeKok left quickly.

6

Vledder looked numb for a moment.

"We're named in a complaint," he repeated, shocked, "for illegal entry and trespass?"

"Yes."

Vledder put his head on his desk in despair.

"We've had it coming. How many times have we talked about Handie Henkie's little gadget getting us into trouble? Now we're the subject of an uproar."

DeKok dismissed the criticism.

"The uproar would be legitimate, if I had ever picked a lock for personal reasons. I have only used it to serve the purposes of justice ... and truth."

Vledder snorted.

"Great. How will that help us in the courts?"

Again DeKok shrugged nonchalantly.

"Dick, I'm not all that worried about the courts. I told the commissaris I would respond to the complaint, but only when it is executed and presented, personally, by Mr. Vreeden."

Vledder didn't know whether to be relieved. "How is that possible?"

"What do you mean?"

"Can we just ignore the complaint filed by that Meturovski guy?"

DeKok nodded.

"I think so. We are within our rights to file an objection to the complaint. We have several legitimate reasons. Undoubtedly Meturovski has been delegated to appear for the company in judicial matters. I don't really know whether he's an in-house attorney or outside counsel. Regardless he can act legally only with regard to company matters. Illegal entry, just to name the beast, did not occur on company property. With regard to alleged illegal entry, or trespass, the owner of the premises has to file the complaint himself. Mr. Vreeden is the owner of the home. He has to declare that the entry was illegal, ergo, against his will and without his invitation. He can authorize a lawyer to act for him. But the lawyer would have to have been engaged to address this specific matter. We do not have to acknowledge or accept this as valid from a general power-of-attorney from a corporation." He smiled briefly. It had been a long speech for DeKok. "Please understand," he continued, "my actions were countering, challenging the opposition to produce a live Mr. Vreeden."

Vledder looked worried.

"High stakes," he said looking troubled.

"How's that?"

"If Mr. Vreeden is enjoying good health and good times in the Bahamas, comes home and files a complaint ... then what?"

DeKok laughed carelessly.

"In that case, the famous detective duo of Vledder and DeKok will cease to exist." He grimaced. "We could always start a private detective business."

Vledder looked as if he had smelled something distasteful.

"Oh, good—we'll be testifying in divorce cases about

who is going to bed with whom." His voice dripped with sarcasm.

"Something like that."

Vledder shook his head.

"No thanks, DeKok! I went into police work for a reason—civil cases bore me to death."

DeKok understood his young colleague's apprehension. He smiled reassuringly.

"First we have nothing to prove. The complainants must prove Mr. Vreeden did not call me to discuss serious difficulties at the firm's offices. Then they'll have to prove the front door of Vreeden' villa was locked." There was a twinkle in his eyes. "That may be rather difficult without producing Vreeden."

"They can check phone records."

"Come on. An intelligent man such as Mr. Vreeden would contact me from a phone booth or by wireless, directly to a dedicated line."

"What if he's alive?"

DeKok shook his head.

"He simply is not alive. This complaint only strengthens my conviction."

"I don't get you."

DeKok spread both arms.

"My intimation to the butler regarding Mr. Vreeden's apparent death precipitated the complaint. Our opposition, the people who want us to believe Mr. Vreeden is alive, became nervous. They needed a way to block the investigation."

"They took their best shot," Vledder continued, "a formal complaint against us on the grounds the butler gave them illegal entry and trespass. Whether or not the charges would stick they hoped our superiors would take us off the case."

DeKok gave Vledder an admiring look.

"You're right on target. Keep this up and I'll be able to take early retirement."

"Stuff it," said Vledder.

DeKok grinned and turned around. He picked his hat up off the floor. Vledder eyed his movements with suspicion.

"Where do you think you're going?" he asked.

DeKok, already on his way to the door, looked over his shoulder.

"It's time to have a talk with Fat Nellie Benson. Maybe she knows something about Black Archie's whereabouts."

They waved goodbye to the watch commander as they left the building. They walked down Warmoes Street, turning off into the Red Light District. Warmoes Street was just on the edge of the infamous district. It formed an informal border between the respectable and tawdry. The seamier of the two neighborhoods was the one sought by millions of tourists and sailors.

At this early hour the neighborhood offered a different look from the evening, when the streets were crowded almost beyond capacity. The owners of sex shops were washing their windows. A butcher in wooden shoes and bloody apron scrubbed the street in front of his shop. Even here the Dutch kept their reputation for cleanliness. Windows had to be cleaned and pavements had to be scrubbed. People deposited their trash neatly in the municipal containers.

Only a few prostitutes were behind their windows. Most busied themselves vacuuming, dusting, or washing windows. Vledder stopped involuntarily, as a semi-nude, young woman climbed a ladder to dust the top of the curtain rod inside the window. Since the curtain was opened and closed dozens of times during the night to signal the need for privacy or the availability of the lady behind the glass, he wondered how dust would gather.

DeKok had outdistanced his partner in long strides. Vledder hastened to catch up.

"Are you also investigating Archie's disappearance?" asked Vledder when he had caught up with his partner.

DeKok lifted his head to greet a prostitute with a shopping bag. She daintily tripped into the butcher shop. The woman smiled at DeKok, who was probably the most recognizable figure in the district.

DeKok watched the woman disappear into the shop before he answered.

"That's Blonde Josie, daughter of Pale Goldie. You remember? Goldie's murder was the first case we handled together. Too bad she followed in her mother's footsteps. Let's hope she'll be able to retire in good health and not be killed like her mom."

Vledder turned around, but the young woman had disappeared from view.

"What about Archie?" he repeated his question.

"Little Lowee asked me to look into the disappearance," DeKok answered. "I owe him one."

Vledder grinned hesitantly.

"Aren't we going to be stretching ourselves a bit thin? I'd have thought Vreeden's disappearance would be enough to keep us busy."

DeKok suddenly stopped.

"Have you not wondered what sort of body Archie was talking about?" he demanded.

Vledder was irked.

"You asked that before."

"I ask you again. What kind of body would someone be looking to hide?"

Vledder stared at his partner momentarily. Suddenly his face cleared and his mouth fell open.

"A murder victim, of course—you're surely not thinking it could have been Vreeden's body?" He thought a while. "It may be farfetched, but not impossible," he conceded.

DeKok pushed his hat back on his head and strolled toward Old Church Square, taking the bridge across to Old Acquaintance Alley. DeKok could find his way through Old Amsterdam blindfolded. He knew all the shortcuts, ancient bridges, and narrow, obscure alleys. Even a city planner would have had to consult old maps and drawings to find the way through this maze. This was DeKok's turf; he knew every step, house, and almost every prostitute behind each window.

Eventually they reached Mill Alley. Vledder followed, his head bent in thought. New perspectives began to occur to him.

"If we could just get Archie Benson to talk," he thought suddenly out loud.

DeKok ignored the remark.

He stopped again at Mill Alley, just a few houses away from Seadike. His eyes traveled from the brightly painted door, up the façade, to a window. There was a spy mirror attached to the outside of the window. When he saw movement reflected there, he pressed open the door and hoisted his two hundred pounds up the narrow staircase. Vledder waited a moment before following, two steps at a time.

At the top of the stairs there was a short corridor.

DeKok rested a moment. When his breathing was back to normal, he knocked on a door and entered.

A corpulent woman was seated at the table. There was a steaming bowl in front of her and she had a tea towel over her head. She took the tea towel away and looked up.

The old inspector smiled.

"What are you doing, Nell?"

The woman pointed at the bowl.

"Chamomile," she explained. A stubby finger tapped her forehead. "I'm all plugged up here. I think I have a cold."

"No good comes from standing in front of a drafty door in the middle of the night."

Her face became hard.

"You have career advice for me?"

DeKok sidestepped the question.

"What do you hear from Archie?" he asked with concern.

She shook her head. Her face began to lose its angry flush.

She answered, dejectedly, "My boy has been missing for five days now. My first thought was the cops had him in custody for one thing or another. That's why I asked Lowee to check with you."

"You could have come yourself."

"I don't like going to the station."

DeKok shook his head with a sigh.

"We're not holding your son anywhere. We also checked the hospitals—he hasn't been hospitalized, either." He paused. "Does he have a new girlfriend?"

She leaned back and buttoned her blouse.

"Plenty of girls," she said carelessly. "But not one

who would keep him from stopping by to see his mother every day."

"How about work—was he doing a job for anyone?"

"I don't know, don't think so."

DeKok scrutinized her closely.

"Maybe he has a new partner?"

She did not answer at once, but stared at the bowl of steaming water.

"Archie," she said finally, "Archie has never had a father. About twenty years ago I got to know an Englishman. He was a dark, good-looking guy with plenty of money. He said he had taken part in a, now famous, train robbery in England. He had fled to Holland. Well, you could guess the rest. He was going to get me out of the business, marry me. I became pregnant with Archie and he slunk away into the night, never to be seen again." She paused. Her right hand searched for a pack of cigarettes on the table. "For the last few weeks Archie has been obsessed with a new acquaintance. He met an older man, around forty-five ..... Maybe he's some sort of substitute father."

"What's the name of this new acquaintance?"

Nellie spread her plump hands.

"I don't know."

DeKok did not believe her.

"But Archie obviously discussed him with you."

Fat Nellie nodded vaguely.

"Archie calls him Buck Jones. Of course, it's an alias or a street name. I don't even know, for sure, he's in the business, you know. It's just a suspicion. Archie has been very close mouthed about it. It's almost as if the guy has some sort of power over Archie. Normally Archie doesn't keep things that close to his chest."

"Has he ever been here?"

Nell shook her head.

"I wanted to invite him, but Archie wasn't having any of it."

"You have never seen him?"

She lit a cigarette, inhaled deeply, and then extinguished it immediately in an ashtray.

She exhaled some smoke. "I caught a glimpse of him at a distance. He waited at the corner of Seadike, while Archie stopped to see me for a moment." She stared again at the bowl of now cooling water. "And you know what's so strange?"

"Well?"

"There was something strangely familiar about him."

"You'd seen him before?"

Fat Nellie shrugged.

"I don't know. I might have met him sometime ago, maybe as a john."

"Can you give a description?"

Nell smiled sadly.

"I told you. I just saw him for a moment. I can't remember what he looked like."

DeKok sighed deeply.

"You must have gotten something," he said patiently. "Where does he live? Where did he go with Archie? Were there other friends ... accomplices?"

She looked up at him.

"He has a tattoo on his left arm."

"How did you find that out?"

"One day Archie showed me his left arm. He had a sword tattooed on his arm in blue and red. It was like a knight's sword, with a long handle and a knob at the end. I didn't approve—thought it was ugly. When I asked Archie why he got the tattoo, he told me Buck has one just like it."

DeKok glanced at Vledder, who was busily scribbling in his notebook.

"Could this man, Buck, have had anything to do with Archie's disappearance?"

Fat Nellie made a helpless gesture. Her lower lip started to tremble. Suddenly she took the old man's hand.

"I don't know," she said in a shaky voice. "Mr. DeKok, I'm so afraid … I'm so afraid something bad has happened to Archie." She moved in her chair and pointed at a telephone on the sideboard. By now she was blubbering. "Last night someone called here, a man. He asked whether I had a life insurance policy for Archie. I said, 'Since the day he was born.'" She took a deep breath. Big tears rolled over her cheeks. "Then the man said …" She did not finish the sentence and burst out in heartrending sobbing.

DeKok put a consoling hand on her shoulder.

"What did the man say?" he asked in a soft voice.

Nell's teary face looked at him.

"He said, 'You can tear up that policy.' Then he hung up."

7

They left the narrow Mill Alley and turned the corner on Seadike. Seadike is not a dike at all, but the name of a street. Hundreds of years ago, it *was* a dike. It also marked the city limits of Amsterdam. Through the years ongoing land reclamation and growth pushed the dike to the middle of the city. As houses and shops were built on either side the dike became another thoroughfare.

There was an angry snarl around Vledder's mouth. "What a dirty, heartless act," he said with genuine anger. "What kind of person makes that kind of a call to a worried mother?" He looked at his partner. "What sort of low-life does that?"

DeKok shrugged.

"I can't say."

"Do you think it was a sick joke by someone who knows Archie has been missing?"

DeKok shook his head slowly.

"I'm afraid not," he said gloomily. "I don't think that call was a joke at all. It was some cynical individual, who chose that way to tell Nellie her son was dead."

"Then you think the caller knew?"

"Of course," agreed DeKok. "The only question is how he came by the information. Did he hear it from someone?"

"Or is he responsible for the death?" finished Vledder.

"That's right. Instinct and experience lead me to this new cohort of Archie's. Nellie believed her son was deeply influenced by this virtual stranger. I have to wonder whether he has something to do with Archie's disappearance, possibly, his death."

"What's-his-name with the tattoo?"

DeKok nodded.

"There would have been no risk to him in making the call. Archie never introduced him to Fat Nellie, so she wouldn't know his voice." He walked on for awhile in silence. "I can't shake the feeling there was a reason why Archie declined to take his new partner home to Mother," he said after about a dozen steps. "He's not just in the shadows. He's a sinister figure in the background of all this."

Vledder cleared his throat.

"Surely we should be able to locate a guy like this."

"The man seems to guard his identity carefully. You can surmise as much from Nellie's story."

"Why would he have gotten involved with Archie, who's not all that bright, according to Lowee?"

DeKok grimaced.

"He needed him for something, I think. Archie was available. He was extraordinarily willing. He was amenable; he'd follow orders without thinking too much."

"For instance, he could help dispose of a body unofficially, so to speak."

"For instance," nodded DeKok. "The question is, if Archie is dead, why did he die? What changed?"

They continued to walk, apparently, in no particular direction. A heavily built man approached them near Short Storm Alley. The gray sleuth stopped with a smile on his face.

"Handsome Karl," exclaimed DeKok. "I've missed you for some time."

The man grinned cheerfully.

"True. I took a few months vacation, at the state's expense. The Hague cops nabbed me after a burglary in a villa."

"You can't be serious," said DeKok. "You got nabbed by out-of-town police? Where's your civic pride?"

"Sometimes a person needs to expand his horizons. Anyway, I didn't like their jail. They didn't speak my language. But I'm glad we ran into each other. I just came from Warmoes Street. I asked for you, but they told me you were out."

"What can I do for you, Karl?"

"I talked to Little Lowee. He steered me your way."

"What for?"

"It's about Archie, Black Archie. Lowee said Archie has gone missing and you have the case."

DeKok nodded.

"What can you tell me about Archie?"

Karl shrugged.

"Not much, but Lowee seemed to think it's important. A few nights ago I met Archie on Rear Fort Canal. We know each other fairly well. You see, I knew his mother a long time before. We set up housekeeping together once, before she became Fat Nellie. She was a lot of woman in her day. Anyway, you understand, Archie trusts me."

"And?"

Handsome Karl suddenly seemed bashful. He scratched the back of his neck.

"Archie acted a bit strange. He's not usually so nervous. He was biting his nails a lot. Suddenly he asked me if I ever had to get rid of a corpse. I said I hadn't ... that's the truth. I've never been into violence of any kind. The kid came out and asked where I thought would be the best place to bury a corpse."

DeKok looked at him intently.

"And what kind of advice did you give him?"

"I told him the Kemner Dunes."

DeKok's face remained expressionless.

"Why there?"

Karl looked away.

"There's a lot of loose sand there, and I've heard—somewhere—it would be easy to 'lose' a body there."

"And what did Archie say? Was he seeing it as a possibility?"

Karl grimaced.

"He asked me the best way to get there in a car. I told him to take the Sea Path from Bloemendaal along the beach. There are some thick bushes. It would be pretty easy to dig there without being noticed." He hastily added, "I know, because my parents used to have a little summer cottage there."

DeKok shook his head in disapproval.

"You never bothered to ask why he needed to get rid of a body?"

Handsome Karl looked irritated.

"Why should I? Some things you don't want to know."

"Why not?"

Karl sighed deeply.

"Archie was obviously in trouble," he explained, patiently. "I didn't mind helping him, but I wasn't going to risk jail by becoming an accomplice. I try to be careful, you see? I was fresh out of jail, myself. If Archie got himself involved with a murder or an execution somehow, he was old enough to wipe his own backside."

"Did he ask for your help?"

"No, he didn't, not directly. He did say it was important not to have the body turn up. 'It's important they never find him,' he said."

"He said *him* and *they*?"

"Yes."

"So it was the body of a man."

Karl spread his hands, palms up.

"DeKok, please don't involve me in any of this. Believe me, I only talked to the boy for a few minutes. I cut it off as soon as I could. I simply did not, and do not, want to know anything more." There was a pleading look in his eyes. "You can understand that, can't you, DeKok?"

The hard look on the inspector's face faded away and became milder. He put a hand on Karl's shoulder.

"Why don't you go back to Fat Nellie one of these days? She could use a friend right now."

The inspectors entered the station house at Warmoes Street. Meindert Post was the watch commander. Like DeKok he was born on the island of Urk. Unlike DeKok he had retained his loud fisherman's voice. Post always sounded as if he were trying to reach the ears of someone on the bow of a ship in a gale.

"DeKok!!" he roared.

The sound reverberated against the walls.

DeKok pushed his hat farther back on his hat and ambled over to the counter. He had known Meindert Post for more then twenty-five years and he was still surprised by the volume of his voice. DeKok leaned against the counter toward the watch commander.

"Meindert," he said sweetly, "did you call me?"

Post gesticulated, momentarily at a loss for words.

"You're always gone," he growled finally. "You can never be reached. I know you don't use walkie-talkies, but you could allow Vledder to keep in touch by radio, couldn't you?"

In his own way, Meindert was just as old-fashioned as DeKok. The police had long since abandoned walkie-talkies in favor of minuscule communication devices that looked somewhat like clip-on cell phones.

DeKok grinned pleasantly.

"Fish we catch at sea," he said. "I can't catch them in the office. You, of all people, should know unnecessary noise scares the fish."

"Oh, all right, Handsome Karl was here, looking for you."

DeKok pushed himself away from the counter.

"Old news—we ran into him."

"And there's a lady waiting for you, upstairs."

DeKok had a questioning look.

"What kind of lady?"

Meindert Post raised his hand and pressed the thumb and index finger together.

"First class."

DeKok shook his head.

"Way out of my league, yours, too," he joked. "Nevertheless, she asked for you. When I told her you were out, she insisted on waiting for you."

With a shrug, DeKok turned to climb the stairs.

Vledder followed.

A woman was seated on the bench in the corridor, near the entrance of the detective room. DeKok figured her to be about forty years old. She wore an expensively cut, wine-red suit. A pure-white, silk scarf set off her olive skin. Large, almond eyes twinkled in an oval face. Her jet-black hair had been combed back and pulled together in a chignon, held in place by diamond-studded golden hairpins.

The old inspector beheld her with approval. Meindert Post, he thought, hit the nail on the head. He approached her and bowed with the elegance and elan of a former era.

"You are waiting for me?"

She looked up at him, but gave the impression she was looking down with a hauteur that seemed natural.

"You're Inspector DeKok?"

"With a kay-oh-kay," he replied automatically.

She smiled faintly.

"They told me that would be your reaction."

"Who are *they*?"

She waved that away as unimportant.

"Friends," she evaded, "some friends advised me to consult you."

DeKok did not press her. He held open the door and accompanied her to the chair next to his desk.

"Please have a seat."

She sat down carefully, crossed her slender legs, and pulled the skirt of her suit down over her knees.

"My name is Xaveria, Xaveria Breerode. I've been Paul Vreeden's friend for a number of years. He's why I've come to see you"

"Who did you say?"

She looked surprised.

"Paul Vreeden," she repeated. "Do you know him?"

DeKok shook his head.

"No, no. I mean … I've never met him, I did hear his name mentioned in connection with a dredging company."

Xaveria nodded agreement.

"Yes, that's Paul. He's the managing director of the firm. Paul and I have an understanding, a so-called LAT relationship. We choose to live by ourselves. We only get together on the weekends. We never meet in Bergen, where Paul owns a comfortable villa. He doesn't want me to come there. We always get together in Amersfoort, where I own a condominium. Paul prefers to keep our relationship private. He never wants to appear with me in public. We never go out together."

DeKok cocked his head at her.

"Why not?" he asked, surprised. "I'd be proud to be seen with you."

Xaveria gave him a tinkling laugh.

"Paul is very well-regarded in his circle. He's a world-renowned expert on the design, construction, and maintenance of waterways and harbors. It's never been an issue, but his public persona is that of a confirmed bachelor."

DeKok gave her a searching look.

"Why are you telling me this?"

Her face fell.

"I came to see you because I'm very worried. I'm afraid something has happened to him."

"What do you think has happened?"

Xaveria raised her hands in a gesture of desperation.

"I don't know what to think. Everything is so surreal." She looked at DeKok and the old man read fear in her eyes. "Paul comes every Friday night about seven o'clock.

Last Friday he did not show up. We had talked to each other the day before. He telephoned me. Our conversation was normal. We caught up with each other, chatted about this and that. By nine o'clock the following Friday I had not heard from him, so I phoned his house. There was no answer. I stayed home all weekend long, waiting for some news. It was no use—he never called or came." She took a deep breath and her fingers twisted her scarf. "The weekend passed this way. On Monday morning I called his office at exactly nine o'clock. His secretary told me that Mr. Vreeden could not be reached. He was on vacation in the Bahamas."

DeKok looked dismayed.

"But that's possible, isn't it?"

She shook her head.

"Paul would never do that."

"Do what?"

"Leave without telling me."

DeKok nodded thoughtfully.

"So, you don't believe he went to the Bahamas?"

"No."

"What *do* you believe?"

Xaveria Breerode lowered her head. Her lips trembled.

"I think he's been kidnapped."

8

DeKok now looked skeptical.

"Kidnapped?" he repeated. "What makes you think that?"

Xaveria looked up.

"Paul had been warned."

DeKok made an effort to be expressionless.

"Someone warned him he would be kidnapped?" he asked, after a long pause. The disbelief in his voice was genuine.

"Yes," said Xaveria. "About a month ago he received a phone call. It was a young man, who told him he was going to be kidnapped. He said the preparations were almost complete."

"What did Paul say about this young man?"

She shook her head.

"Paul didn't recognize the voice. Paul thought it was a young man's voice. Whoever it was didn't give a name, but he warned Paul not to tell anybody. He said, 'They may kill me if you say anything.'"

DeKok nodded. He glanced at Vledder. The young inspector was quietly typing on his computer keyboard. DeKok didn't doubt Vledder was recording the conversation verbatim. Vledder had a new, auxiliary keyboard. It allowed him to enter stenographers' codes into his computer.

DeKok did not think the codes could be automatically transcribed, but nothing would surprise him in this day and age.

"Did Mr. Vreeden take the warning as serious?" he resumed his questioning.

"Absolutely."

"Did he warn the police or take any preventive measures, step up security?"

"No," she sighed. "That's not Paul's way. I'm sorry to have to tell you this. He hasn't much faith in the police. Even so he won't hire a bodyguard. Aside from his obvious energies and talents, he's a conservative, uncomplicated man. Maybe that's what I love about him. He insists on an outdated ritual when he goes abroad on business. He is known to travel with large amounts of cash in a money vest. When he gets where he's going to negotiate a contract, he distributes 1,000 Euro bills like it is Christmas. Call him crazy, but he always comes back with multi-million dollar contracts."

DeKok smiled.

"Is he wealthy?"

Xaveria pursed her lips in thought before she answered.

"Paul is financially well off," she said in the hesitant manner of the very rich. "He has a very comfortable net worth, but almost all his wealth is in the company."

DeKok looked thoughtfully in the distance.

"Should we assume for the moment that Mr. Vreeden has indeed been kidnapped, who would his abductors most likely contact for ransom?"

The company would get the call. The people who would be able to make a decision to pay ransom are the co-directors, Messrs. Grauw and Middelkoop."

"Do you know the two gentlemen?"

She shook her head.

"I've never met them."

"Do they know about your ... eh, your relationship with Mr. Vreeden?"

"I doubt it. As we discussed, Paul didn't want our relationship known. He would not have discussed it in the office."

"Would they pay a considerable amount of ransom?"

Xaveria seemed genuinely surprised.

"Why do you ask?"

DeKok looked dubious.

"The motive for paying a ransom, regardless of the amount, is emotional attachment. Close, loving ties are the reason kidnappers contact the victim's family. In a business setting, personal attachments are rare."

Xaveria Breerode looked at him as if he were a being from another world. Then her dark eyes sparked malevolently.

"Emotional attachment, Mr. DeKok, has no bearing here. Mr. Vreeden is worth his weight in gold to the company."

After Xaveria had left, Vledder slapped his forehead.

"This is getting crazier by the minute," he exclaimed. He looked at DeKok. "Aren't you ready to abandon ship?"

"What?"

"Maybe we shouldn't get sucked in any farther!"

"Why?"

The young inspector grimaced.

"I can't remember a crazier case during all the time we've worked together. It just keeps getting crazier."

"You said that," interrupted DeKok.

"And I'll probably say it again. What about Handsome Karl's story? Here we go again—what can we do? Start digging in the dunes with a bulldozer?"

DeKok laughed.

"I don't think the authorities will allow it. The dunes are protected, you know. They are our only protection from the sea in places where there are no dikes. Where would you start? Besides how would you justify the sacrilege? Tell them that we think we're looking for the corpse of someone who's on vacation in the Bahamas? We haven't even tied Archie's corpse to the missing Mr. Vreeden."

Vledder was a little insulted.

"I know all that about the dunes. I just brought it up as an illustration of insurmountable problems with this case," he said. He glanced at his computer screen, as if for inspiration. Then he added, "Are you now saying Archie's corpse and Vreeden are *not* one and the same?"

DeKok shook his head, becoming more serious.

"We can't ignore the possibility. But it's too soon for it to be our sole theory, and we haven't anything concrete. Of course I'm deeply concerned about the disappearance and the possible death of Archie. Unfortunately Archie's fate is just as obscure as Vreeden's."

Vledder looked at his screen again, pensively.

"By the way," he said after a long pause, "I didn't want to interrupt while you were talking with Xaveria, but what is a LAT relationship?"

DeKok scratched the back of his neck.

"It's just another example of how English is creeping into our language. It stands for *Living Alone Together.*"

"Sounds like an oxymoron."

"What?" asked DeKok. He was thinking of something else.

"Together living apart?"

DeKok shrugged.

"You heard her. Xaveria's and Paul's relationship works for them."

"And what about her story of the threatened kidnapping?"

Again DeKok shrugged. Something was nagging at him, but he could not quite grasp it.

"We have had a few widely publicized, high-profile kidnap cases. It wouldn't be so farfetched for the renowned, wealthy Mr. Vreeden to be a potential victim."

Vledder consulted his screen again, while he made a few entries in his notebook.

"According to Xaveria," he said with emphasis, "Vreeden was actually warned. The caller said the plan to kidnap him was almost complete."

DeKok merely nodded.

Vledder continued, "The so-called warning doesn't ring true, unless it could have been a sick joke or a red herring."

DeKok hesitated before he answered.

"It's a stretch. But we can't rule out the possibility there was a plan to kidnap Vreeden. His mystery caller could have been someone with an axe to grind, someone who knew about a conspiracy. If it was someone who had a lot to lose it would explain why he also warned Vreeden not to talk."

Vledder swallowed

"'They may kill me if you say anything,'" he read from his notes on the screen.

The words echoed through the room.

The two inspectors fell silent, each immersed in his own thoughts. Vledder stood up and walked over to DeKok's desk. It was just a few steps. Then he turned around and went back to his own desk. But he did not sit down. Suddenly he turned and faced DeKok.

"In spite of Xaveria's story we can dismiss the kidnapping theory. Vreeden was *not* kidnapped. He was found dead in his chair." Then he hesitated and looked at DeKok with doubt on his face. "Or ... not?" he asked, as an afterthought.

DeKok did not answer. He thought about the two of them sitting, exchanging theories, and asking questions. How much police work was done in this manner? He smiled, thinking about Lowee's cop coop joke. The little barkeep had a point. He and Vledder did resemble brooding chickens; they brooded over questions of life and death.

Before he had formulated an answer for Vledder, there was a knock on the door of the detective room. One of the detectives near the door yelled, "Come in." A young man opened the door. He took a moment to speak with the detective who had called for him to come in. The officer pointed in the direction of DeKok and Vledder. The young man thanked him and approached DeKok's desk.

DeKok estimated his age at around twenty-five years. He was dressed in a pair of stained, corduroy pants and a leather jacket with a torn sleeve. He stood still in front of DeKok's desk.

"Are you in charge of the Archie Benson case?" he asked.

DeKok nodded.

"With whom do I have the pleasure?"

The young man smiled. His open face under the disordered blond hair revealed a sunny disposition.

"My name is Kees ... Kees Wallen," he said cheerfully. "I think Little Lowee must have alerted every gangster in Amsterdam. You can't go anywhere without having some goon asking you what you know about Archie."

DeKok looked up at the standing man.

"And ... what do you know about Archie?"

Without waiting for an invitation, Kees Wallen sat down and pushed a packet out of a breast pocket. He selected a cigarette and lit it.

"About two months ago, I sold him a boat," he said through a cloud of cigarette smoke.

A recent ordinance prohibited smoking in the police station, but DeKok said nothing to his guest. In response to a silent signal, Vledder opened one of the windows, disapproval written on his face.

"What kind of boat?" asked DeKok.

"It was a small cabin cruiser. She was old, all wood, but in excellent condition. She had a 40HP Kromhout engine with a glow-head."

Vledder looked surprised.

"That model of engine hasn't been in use for a long time," he remarked.

"Yes," DeKok added without a moment's hesitation. "Aren't those rather old fashioned?"

Vledder looked in surprise at his partner. Usually DeKok avoided all technical discussions. Vledder could have sworn DeKok wouldn't know an antiquated boat engine from today's equivalent. Cars, engines, computers ... it was all "modern" stuff to DeKok.

Wallen didn't notice. He just grinned.

"You might call it a real museum piece."

"And Archie bought it from you?"

The young man nodded.

"I do a little business in boats," he explained.

"And Archie knew that?"

"Sure. He'd bought a boat from me before. It was a little runabout, strictly for fun. He ended up reselling it."

"You don't think he bought the cabin cruiser to resell it?"

Kees Wallen moved uneasily in his chair. The sunny expression left his face.

"I didn't understand," he said somberly. "I just couldn't figure why Archie would be interested in that cabin cruiser. If you wanted to use it for anything but show, it would need a lot of remodeling. An old Kromhout engine like that, for instance, you would have to replace."

DeKok pulled out his lower lip and let it plop back. As usual, he repeated the annoying gesture several times.

"Did Archie say what he planned to do with the boat?"

Kees Wallen shook his head.

"I met him near the canal the day he bought her. He just asked if I had a boat for sale. I said yes and took him to the Old Waal. That's where I kept that cabin cruiser, near the stone bridge. As soon as we got aboard, Archie checked out the cabin and said he'd take it."

"He didn't ask the price?"

Kees grinned slyly.

"No, he never asked." The sun came back on his face. "So, I quickly added a few hundred."

DeKok nodded.

"And he paid?"

"He patted his chest. Archie had a big roll of cash. He paid on the spot."

"Where did he plan to anchor the boat?"

"That I don't know. He must have had it towed. A few days later it was gone."

"Do you know where it wound up?"

"Yes," Wallen nodded slowly. "I found out by chance. About a week ago I met an old friend. He'd sold me the boat in the first place. He asked me if I still owned it. I told him I didn't and he told me he had seen it."

"Where?"

Kees Wallen grinned apologetically.

"On the Amstel ... across from Sorrow Field, the cemetery."

9

They left the station in the battered VW and drove in the direction of the Damrak. The car groaned and protested as Vledder floored the gas pedal to make the green light at the crossing to the dam. DeKok reacted annoyed. He did not like driving and despised sudden accelerations.

"What's the matter?" he growled. "Are we in a hurry to get to hell or the next stoplight?"

Vledder grinned broadly. He enjoyed getting a rush of speed out of the anemic, underpowered vehicle.

"Me?" he wondered. "I'll never go to hell. Just for hanging out with you for so long, I'm guaranteed a seat in heaven."

DeKok shook his head.

"I shouldn't count on it, if I were you. I've been told they refuse all cops at the Pearly Gates."

Vledder laughed.

"Sure. They undoubtedly have ex-police enforcing it."

DeKok grumbled, "Just take it easy. I'm in no rush to go to either place."

"What's this sudden interest in boats," asked Vledder, getting back to business.

"I'm interested in it because Archie bought it, that's all."

"That's it?"

The gray sleuth sank deeper in the seat and pushed back his hat.

"Doesn't the sale of a cabin cruiser to a guy like Archie give you pause," he asked, patiently. For instance, how did Black Archie, whose mother supported him in his adulthood, suddenly come by a big roll of money? If he didn't keep a tiny, pleasure boat, why would he want the cruiser? The timing of the boat deal is interesting, as well. Archie was already under the influence of a stranger, Buck Jones. It makes me wonder whether this Jones character financed the purchase and why.

Vledder was skeptical.

"What do you expect to learn by looking at the boat?"

DeKok spread his hands.

"Maybe nothing," he grimaced. "Or maybe we can lift the tip of the veil surrounding Archie's mysterious disappearance."

Meanwhile Vledder was making good time. He passed the mint, turning right just before Rembrandt Square. They were already approaching the bridge across Gentlemen's Canal.

"Archie's disappearance certainly seems to interest Little Lowee. He sends us everybody who has a little tidbit to offer."

DeKok smiled.

"This is not the first time. I've seen it happen before. When that little nondescript barkeeper uses his influence, things happen. I can assure you it doesn't pay to underestimate Lowee's power."

"Power?" questioned Vledder.

DeKok nodded emphatically.

"Power, yes. Little Lowee knows everybody in the underworld and his knowledge is power. Lowee knows which skeletons are in whose closets."

"Are we talking blackmail?"

That shocked DeKok. He pursed his lips judicially.

"No," he said slowly. "He just knows how to encourage certain shady characters to do and say the right things … to serve justice."

This time Vledder laughed out loud.

"DeKok," he said chuckling, "you'd make a perfect politician. You can put a spin on anything. Of course those crumbs do what Lowee demands. They fear what he knows and they fear his relationship with you."

DeKok shook his head. His face was serious.

"That's not the way it is, at all. My friendship with Lowee is not a factor. I have arrested him more than once. Lowee has done several stretches in jail because of me. Actually guys like Handsome Karl and Kees Wallen already believe one hand washes the other. Don't forget, when they get in trouble, they know Lowee is the first one to help."

They approached the Amstel Dike and drove under the Utrecht Bridge. As they drove along the Amstel River, DeKok pushed himself into an upright position. The view of the beautiful river was spoiled by a collection of derelict barges and neglected houseboats.

"A beautiful city," he sighed, "but that is disgraceful, such disregard for …" He did not complete the sentence.

Vledder smiled to himself. He knew his old friend was dismayed by the blight of neglect. This landscape would otherwise be one of the most idyllic riverfronts anywhere. The laissez-fair attitude of the city council regarding houseboats rankled.

"Do you have some idea what our cabin cruiser looks like?" asked Vledder.

"From Wallen's description I imagine something like a cut-down tourist boat, only shorter. It would be more narrow, and with a cabin running almost from the bow to the stern. However I do know what a Kromhout glow-head engine looks like."

Vledder was surprised.

"I thought you knew nothing about engines. How did you come by this rather technical knowledge?"

DeKok smiled.

"My grandfather was a fisherman. The first real engine I saw in my life was a Kromhout glow-head in his fishing shack. I often watched the burner heat the head of the engine until it was red hot. Only then could Grandfather start the motor."

They slowed down. Just past the cemetery they saw an old cabin cruiser. The wood was weathered, the brass work was tarnished. The iron railing and bollards were rusted. Even the ropes with which it was moored looked black with age.

"That must be it," pointed Vledder.

DeKok nodded. Vledder parked the VW against the cemetery fence and they stepped out of the car. For a moment they just stood next to the car. Dusk was falling. The stretch of Amstel looked deserted. A balmy breeze rustled through the high poplars behind them.

Slowly they crossed the road to the grassy berm. They inspected the spikes that had been driven into the ground to receive the mooring lines. Then they took a closer look at the boat.

Two brand new, shiny brass padlocks glowed amidst all the tarnish, catching their attention. One locked the doors.

The other secured the hatch to the steps that appeared to lead into the boat from the tiny aft deck.

There was no gangway. With difficulty DeKok scrambled from the shore onto the deck of the freeboard around the superstructure. The freeboard ran on both sides of the boat, connecting the narrow aft deck with an even tinier deck over the bow.

DeKok shuffled along the freeboard to a hatch amid ships. He lifted it and looked down into the boat. With a grin he came upright and closed the hatch.

"It's an old Kromhout glow-head. There's no mistaking it."

He came astern and looked at the padlocks.

"And these," he said casually, "are easy as pie."

Vledder looked worried.

"You're not going inside," he whispered in a rasp. "We've got one complaint against us already."

DeKok ignored him. He took out Handie Henkie's instrument and made a few adjustments. Within seconds both locks were open. Vledder watched with a worried expression, but said nothing more.

DeKok pocketed the locks and smiled at his young colleague.

"It's not my fault the law constrains us so," he said, apologetically. He raised a finger in the air. "It isn't like we're creating our own odds; the law is designed more to protect the criminal than to take him out of circulation."

Vledder's face was disapproving.

"That's why you ignore the law?" he said harshly.

"No, Dick," answered DeKok jovially, "I don't. I honor the law and serve justice to the best of my ability." He chuckled. " I admit, sometimes, I'm a bit unconventional."

He turned around and slid back the hasp. He reached down and opened the bolt on the inside of the doors. He pushed the doors wide open to descend the steps into the interior. Right at the bottom of the steps he almost walked into a recently installed partition. In the middle of the partition was a heavy, securely bolted door. He pushed aside the well-oiled bolts and pushed open the door. It was pitch black in the space.

Vledder handed him a flashlight,

 DeKok flashed the beam through the space. It was small, about six by nine feet. There were no windows, no portholes, and the walls were covered with a thick layer of foam rubber. To the left, next to an army cot, was a chemical toilet.

Vledder looked over DeKok's shoulder.

"Someone was kept here."

"Yes," nodded DeKok, "a kidnap victim."

They left the boat and walked back to the car. After some deliberation, DeKok had decided to remove all traces of their presence. He had replaced the padlocks exactly as he found them.

Vledder held open the passenger door. DeKok lowered himself into the seat. He had a grim expression on his face. He felt more obstreperous than confused. The mysterious disappearances of Vreeden and Benson had pushed him into making a number of dubious decisions within a very short timeframe. Throughout his long career he had always had the courage of his convictions. An independent thinker, he was not afraid to take risks. He deviated from orthodox detective methods. He was hardest on himself and had never had occasion to question his personal or professional ethics, until now. He didn't feel so self-assured. The very vagueness surrounding the disappearances made him hesitate to plan new approaches.

When Vledder sat down behind the wheel, DeKok indicated that he should wait before starting the engine.

"I want to talk to you for a moment," he said, somberly. "This concerns you as well."

Vledder looked startled. DeKok's somber tone touched him.

"Go ahead."

DeKok hesitated, looking for the right words.

"Well, first of all, I may have been a bit too casual about the complaint Vreeden's colleague filed. I regret making rash decisions that include you. Your career is ahead of you and I may have put it at risk."

"You mean, besides the allegations in the complaint?"

"I'm referring to what we did on the boat. We just violated police regulations. We threw away the rule book."

"What are you telling me?"

DeKok sighed deeply.

"Kidnapping is a serious crime. One of the worst I can think of. It's right up there with rape and crimes against children ... . By quietly putting everything back in order and leaving we are pretending not to have discovered the place where a kidnap victim may have been imprisoned."

Vledder shrugged.

"We don't know there has been a kidnapping."

"Not yet."

The young inspector smiled condescendingly.

"Well, if we hear about a kidnapping tomorrow, we'll know where to look."

DeKok looked at him through the rearview mirror.

"Oh, yes—where?"

"Right here on this boat."

DeKok closed his eyes momentarily. He couldn't believe his junior's obtuseness.

"A boat in a land surrounded by waterways is movable," he said, chidingly. "There must be thousands of hiding places for a boat in Holland. It could be hidden in plain sight. A few pots of paint can make a huge difference. It isn't even that unique."

Vledder looked abashed.

"You're right—what do we do next?"

DeKok put his head down for a moment.

"The simplest, most obvious thing would be to have it towed to a safe place by the Water Police. We had probable cause to look for Archie and it would be no problem to have it examined as a crime scene."

"Well, sounds like a plan."

DeKok rubbed his chin.

"I can see the headlines: 'Secret Hiding Place for Kidnap Victim Discovered,' and 'Youthful Criminal Disappears Under Mysterious Circumstances.'" A good journalist, like Bram Brakel of *The Telegraph,* can connect the dots and turn this into front-page news."

Vledder grinned.

"Lowee created quite a stir. The street buzz is we're looking for Archie Benson."

"Correct," said DeKok slowly, "only we and the perpetrator or perpetrators know Archie's disappearance may be linked to another disappearance. And that, my dear Dick, is a small advantage I'd like to keep for a while."

Vledder frowned.

"Sooner or later somebody is bound to come back to the boat. What if we put it under surveillance?"

A sad smile played around DeKok's lips for a moment.

"Where are we going to get the manpower? In the old days, when we had plenty of people, it wouldn't have posed a problem." He pointed at the trees. "If necessary we would build a crow's nest in one of those poplars."

Vledder started the beetle.

"DeKok," he said, deferring to his mentor, "whatever you do, I'll stick with you."

DeKok was touched.

"Thank you," he said simply.

The drive back to the station house was at a relatively leisurely pace. Vledder parked behind the station and they sauntered to the front of the building, dragging their feet. As soon as they entered the lobby, Jan Kuster, who had relieved Meindert Post as the watch commander, beckoned them. Kuster was red faced and agitated.

"Good thing you're here." It sounded forthright and relieved.

"What's the matter?" asked DeKok.

"I was just about ready to phone the commissaris."

"Why?'

Kuster licked his dry lips.

"I just got the notification for Homicide, but you weren't here. After all, you guys are the Homicide Department."

"What notification?" asked DeKok, impatiently.

Kuster read from the note in his hand.

"Someone just found a dead woman at Emperor's Canal, 1217 on the top floor."

For a moment DeKok closed his eyes in a silent prayer, hoping against hope that it was not what he suspected.

"Do you have a name?"

"Yes," answered Kuster. "Her name is Marlies van Haesbergen. Apparently she was strangled with a scarf."

10

DeKok looked down at her. She was on her back on a Persian carpet with a blue design. She had apparently fallen next to an easy chair. Her eyes were wide open and a white, silken scarf was wrapped around her tawny neck.

The old detective kneeled next to her. The wrinkled ends of the scarf were bunched up next to her left ear. The killer had evidently approached from the rear, thrown the scarf over her head, and pulled the scarf very tight. The striations in the skin were deep. They attested to the brute strength the strangler used.

DeKok struggled upright. He was gripped by a vague feeling of guilt. Since they had met, he'd known Marlies van Haesbergen was in danger because she had seen Vreeden dead. He had suppressed his worry because the widow had been very circumspect after discovering Vreeden's body. He had hoped her behavior would have guaranteed her safety.

He looked around the room and carefully observed what he saw. The imposing pieces of furniture in the long, rectangular room were four large club chairs in black leather. The décor was conservative, joyless. The walls were covered with dark blue wallpaper, embellished with gold lilies. A few dark paintings in black and bronze frames hung on the walls. The paintings were obscured by the patina of age.

DeKok breathed deeply. There was the smell of mold, death, and decay in the room. The effect was overwhelming.

Vledder was seated at an antique escritoire near a window heavily curtained in blue velour. He rummaged through papers. The light of a low desk lamp caught his hands in the oval beam of the light.

DeKok turned toward the door. A woman stood in the opening, nervously wringing her hands. DeKok guessed she was close to fifty years old. She was tall, thin, and rather plain. DeKok approached her, treading heavily.

"You discovered her?" he asked.

The woman nodded.

"I'm Annette van Haesbergen," her voice quivered nervously. "I'm a niece. I visit my aunt about once a week, usually on Thursdays. It was the most convenient day for both of us." Her lips curled slightly in a wan smile. "I was the only one in the family who still kept some contact with her. Aunt Marlies was a bit eccentric, not very much loved."

DeKok gave her a searching looked and found some similarity between her and the dead woman.

"But, surely, her eccentricity was no reason for family to avoid her."

Annette shook her head.

"On the contrary, I liked her very much. Aunt Marlies was always very resolute, sometimes a bit cutting. Despite her years, she was still very much in possession of her faculties. Her mind was clear and sharp."

"How did you get in?"

"I have a key."

"Is it an office key?"

Annette van Haesbergen looked surprised.

"There is no other way to reach her apartment."

DeKok nodded to himself.

"Did you notice anything unusual?"

"What do you mean?"

"Was the front door of the office closed and locked in the usual way?"

"Certainly."

"And you took the elevator to go upstairs?"

"As always. Everything seemed normal, until I got to Aunt Marlies' door. It was open."

"How did you react?"

She shrugged her narrow, bony shoulders.

"I went in and called to my aunt. There was no immediate answer, but she doesn't always answer right away. I thought she might be checking the offices. She often behaved as if she was still the wife of the concierge. Usually she'd show up in a few minutes."

"But not this time?"

Miss van Haesbergen shook her head.

"When I felt the delay was a bit long, I decided to take a look. I started toward the door. As I walked around the table I suddenly saw her." She closed her eyes and sighed. "I must have been sitting for at least fifteen minutes, just a few feet from her."

DeKok gestured around the room.

"It is rather dark in here."

Annette van Haesbergen nodded in agreement.

"Aunt Marlies didn't like a lot of light—she felt it chased the good spirits away."

"You knew at once she was dead?"

"Yes," she answered evenly. "It was clear she had been murdered."

"What did you do?"

"First I called the police. After that I tried to reach Mr. Vreeden in Bergen. But I had no success. There was no answer. Then I phoned Mr. Grauw. He promised to come at once."

"When is the last time you saw your aunt alive?"

"It was Saturday, Saturday afternoon, around four. I had done some shopping in the city and decided to stop by to see her."

DeKok kept her eyes in his gaze.

"Did your aunt say anything at all to indicate she was in danger?"

The woman looked pensive. After a few seconds she nodded slowly.

"Aunt Marlies seemed preoccupied. When I remarked on it, she spoke to me sharply. She said: 'Strange things happen in this building.'"

"What sort of strange things were happening?"

Again Annette smiled wanly.

"She said, 'Dead people just disappear like *that*,' and she snapped her fingers."

DeKok feigned surprise.

"She said that?"

"Yes."

"Were you alarmed by what she said?"

"No," she said, shaking her head. " As I said, my aunt was a bit eccentric. When I was ready to leave, she came to the door with me and patted me on the shoulder. 'Never mind, child, I'll work it out,' she said."

"Afterward did you speak with anyone about what your aunt had said?"

She shook her head decisively.

"To be honest, I dismissed it. Old people sometimes get delusional. I thought she was imagining things." She bit her lip. "But now she's dead ..." She did not finish the sentence. Tears welled up in her eyes.

There was a noise on the landing. DeKok stepped quickly into the corridor. Dr. Koning approached from the direction of the elevator, followed by two men from the coroner's office. DeKok took off his hat and reached out a hand.

"Thank you for coming right away," said DeKok, shaking hands with the old coroner.

"We happened to be in the neighborhood," said Dr. Koning. He sighed. "We've had another overdose in an abandoned building, another squatter. When we heard the call on the radio, I decided to stop by here, first. I knew you would be here." He shook his head and sighed. "It is so wearing having to witness so many young lives cut short because of drugs."

DeKok led the coroner into the room. Koning took off his old, greenish Garibaldi hat, carefully pulled up his striped pants, and kneeled down next to the victim.

Carefully, with short tugs, he pulled the scarf a little away from the neck. He studied the striations. Then he closed the eyes of the corpse. For a moment he remained next to the corpse. Then he put one hand on the floor. DeKok hastened to help him up. The old man's knees creaked as he stretched.

Koning replaced his hat and then took out a pince-nez from a vest pocket. He took a large silken handkerchief from another pocket and slowly polished the glasses. When the glasses had been cleaned to his satisfaction, he replaced the handkerchief in his pocket, but placed the pince-nez on his nose.

"She's dead," he announced.

"I suspected it," answered DeKok. Under Dutch law a person cannot be considered dead until death has been established by a physician. In the case of a crime victim, only a coroner, who is always a physician, can certify death.

Dr. Koning peered at DeKok.

"Nothing strange about the striations on the neck," he said in his creaky voice. "However the murderer was a person of great strength."

"A man, then?" asked DeKok.

"I couldn't say. By saying the murderer had great strength, I meant in relation to the victim. It could have been either."

The old coroner nodded and once more lifted his hat to pay his respects, and walked out of the room.

As soon as Dr. Koning's figure disappeared, DeKok turned again toward Annette. He placed one arm around her shoulders in a gesture of tenderness.

"I advise you to go home, now," he said in a friendly tone of voice. "That would be best. I will keep you informed, so you'll be able to make funeral arrangements."

She looked at him. Her thin lips formed a tight line and there was an angry glow in her eyes.

"And when will you arrest her killer?"

DeKok looked at her.

"Soon," he said evenly.

Bram Weelen, the police photographer, made his pictures in great haste. He carefully repacked his beloved Hasselblad and disappeared after a brief goodbye.

DeKok ambled over to Kruger, the dactyloscopist, who was studying a slide on which he had transferred some fingerprint impressions.

"Something bothering Bram?"

"How do you mean?"

"He bolted out of here with barely a word."

Kruger made a note on the back of the slide.

"His oldest daughter is in the hospital," said Kruger, "she's about to give birth."

DeKok laughed.

"Bram is going to be a grandfather."

Ben Kruger looked annoyed.

"Is that somehow strange?"

DeKok shook his head.

"No, but I've known Bram since he was a bachelor. *Grandfather* seemed a long way off back then."

Kruger did not react. He was always a bit reserved. The expression on his thin face rarely changed. He carefully gathered his equipment together and, just as carefully, packed it in his suitcase. Then he walked out of the room. At the door he turned around and lifted his suitcase slightly.

"I'll let you know if I find something."

DeKok nodded and waved. He knew Kruger would most likely find anything significant, if there was anything, long before the small army of crime scene investigators descended on the room.

DeKok did not object to the CSI. He was a strict pragmatist, especially when it came to the allocation of manpower. He and Vledder worked their cases with great efficacy. Their team consisted of Weelen, the photographer, Kruger, the finger print expert, and specialists such as Dr.

Koning and the pathologist. There was also an occasional part-time associate chosen seemingly at random from the available offices. This group had solved more murders in less time than the homicide squad at Headquarters, together with all the CSI officers. DeKok's unorthodox methods made it unlikely he'd be promoted, but his track record ensured he would never be fired.

While these thoughts went fleetingly through his mind, he motioned to the morgue attendants to indicate they could remove the corpse. Silently they placed the stretcher next to the body. With deft movements they opened the body bag and placed the corpse in it. They put the body bag on the stretcher, covered it with a blanket, and secured it with the straps. Still without speaking, they each lifted an end of the stretcher and walked away.

The old inspector had observed the silent, efficient actions of the morgue attendants many times, in similar circumstances. The sight fascinated him. It was as if they carried an actor offstage, while the curtain was still up. The sight was, somehow, more solemn than the last voyage to the grave. The sight of the attendants with their swaying stretcher often plagued him in his dreams. His other recurrent nightmare placed him at the center of a murder investigation he never seemed able to solve.

He banished his depressing thoughts and turned around to look at Vledder. The young inspector came closer, a half-filled plastic bag in his hand. DeKok looked at it.

"What is all this?"

"I think Marlies van Haesbergen saved everything. I put it all in this plastic kitchen bag, postcards, letters, theater tickets, cancelled train tickets. There'll be time to sort through everything in the office."

DeKok nodded vaguely.

"Is the ticket there?"

"What ticket?"

"Remember the ticket to the Bahamas, the one I saw her buy at the travel agency?"

Vledder shook his head.

"I didn't see it."

"Did you look carefully?"

"I emptied all the drawers and compartments."

"What about the secret compartment?"

Vledder looked dumbfounded.

"What secret compartment?"

"Those old cabinets and escritoires often have secret compartments." He grinned. "In a more romantic time, the lady of the house used to hide her clandestine love letters there."

He walked around Vledder and looked carefully at the escritoire. It was, he observed, an exquisite work of art by a talented cabinetmaker.

It was not the first time DeKok had searched for a secret compartment in an old piece of furniture. He knew how to proceed.

He began by removing all the drawers, carefully opening each of the doors. He looked again, patiently. After a while he discovered a movable panel. The wood was slightly worn from use, leaving a faint trace of a groove. When he pushed gently on the small panel, a narrow compartment became visible. It contained a brown envelope. DeKok took it out and unfolded it.

Vledder looked over his shoulder.

"The ticket."

DeKok nodded.

"There is an address, here, as well—Mr. Vreeden, Hotel Out Island Inn, Georgetown, Great Exuma."

Vledder dropped the plastic bag in shock.

"Then he *is* alive," he panted, "in the Bahamas."

11

Vledder grinned without mirth.

"This isn't happening—how is it possible?" He looked at DeKok.

DeKok did not answer. He studied the address. It was written in a spiky handwriting on an unlined piece of notepaper. He showed it to Vledder.

"Is that her handwriting?"

The younger inspector nodded slowly.

"I think so," he said pensively. "I found quite a few things in her desk written in the same handwriting."

DeKok replaced the ticket and the note in the brown envelope.

"That address," he said sadly, "must have prompted her to go to the travel agency and book a trip."

"To see how a dead Mr. Vreeden spends his holidays."

DeKok glanced at Vledder. For Vledder the remark sounded cynical, but it touched something in DeKok.

"Exactly," he said in a moody voice. "To see how a dead Mr. Vreeden spends his holidays." He placed the brown envelope in an inner pocket and felt for the passport he had found in Bergen. "Everybody around her maintained that Vreeden was on vacation in the Bahamas. She knew what she saw, but the trauma and the contradiction shook her confidence. She must have felt a need to resolve the dichotomy. Remember what she told her niece: *'Never mind, child, I'll work it out.'*"

Vledder shook his head in sympathy.

"It meant her death."

DeKok nodded.

"And the murderer had to work fast. There was little time. He had to act tonight. The ticket is for tomorrow."

Vledder frowned.

"But who knew? I mean who besides us and the people at the travel agency? She wouldn't have told anyone else she planned to head for the Bahamas."

DeKok rubbed his chin.

"How did Marlies get Mr. Vreeden's address?"

"She stole it!"

The inspectors looked up. It was a strange voice. The sound came from behind them. They turned around. A tall, slender man stood in the door opening.

He approached them with a slow, slight limp.

"She stole it," he repeated, nodding his head. "That old woman was always rummaging through the papers in the office. She's done it for years."

He stopped a short distance from the inspectors and placed one hand on a hip, his legs slightly spread.

"We caught her any number of times. Mr. Vreeden always protected her. She should have been packed off to an old-age home long ago. If it had been up to me she'd have never had another opportunity to snoop."

DeKok looked suspiciously at the man. He was forty-ish, dressed in a fashionable gray suit with light blue shirt and burgundy tie. His short, sandy hair was graying at the temples. His face, narrow with high cheekbones and a hawk's nose, didn't add to his likeability.

"And who are you?" asked Vledder.

The man smiled an arrogant smile.

"My name is Grauw, Gerard Grauw. I'm one of the directors of Dredging Works Vreeden. About half an hour ago, I was called by a woman who said that something had happened to her aunt, Mrs. van Haesbergen. She said it was serious."

DeKok narrowed his eyes.

"How long have you been standing in the door?"

Gerard Grauw had an implacable look.

"Long enough. Please go on with your interesting conversation."

DeKok's face became a mask of steel. Ordinarily placid, DeKok could rarely be brought to rage. This was one of those dangerous moments. DeKok was a true Dutchman. The berserker rage of his Batavian forebears was always under the surface.

"Perhaps you should understand," said DeKok, evenly, "the elderly Mrs. van Haesbergen has been strangled to death with a scarf."

"Shocking."

"That's it?" asked DeKok.

"Whatever *do* you mean?"

"That's it? Shocking? That's the only comment you have to make about her death?"

Grauw looked surprised.

"What did you expect?" he asked, with more than a hint of sarcasm. "You expected the rending of garments, sackcloth, and ashes? The old crone was nothing to me, other than a thorn in my side. For years she took up space in prime real estate we own."

DeKok stared at him in disbelief.

"You mean the penthouse apartment, here?"

Grauw nodded.

"The company should either have the space or the income. Aside from the loss of revenue, our offices are increasingly overcrowded."

"So, her death is not unwelcome?"

Grauw pursed his lips and considered the question.

"You might put it that way," he agreed, approval in his voice.

DeKok suppressed an overpowering urge to bash his fists into the narrow face. It wasn't easy; he could see himself rearranging the hawk's nose. He pressed his nails into the palms of his hands, gradually regaining his self-control. Vledder recognized the symptoms. He breathed a silent sigh of relief when DeKok regained his composure.

"You alluded to thefts. You knew Mrs. van Haesbergen had Mr. Vreeden's address on Great Exuma?"

Grauw nodded anew.

"Yes. I can tell you it caused a lot of commotion this morning."

"What kind of commotion?"

Mr. Grauw waved behind his back in the direction of the corridor.

"Karin Peters is very upset."

"Do we know who that is?"

"Karin is Mr. Vreeden's secretary. The old lady had been making a pest of herself. She kept insisting she speak personally with Mr. Vreeden. It had something to do with her apartment. Karin patiently explained, several times, that Mr. Vreeden was not available because he was on vacation in the Bahamas."

"And?"

"This morning she came again. It must have been the fourth time in a single week. Karin explained yet again. When she said Mr. Vreeden was still on vacation, the old woman became furious. She screamed, 'You are lying. He's not on vacation at all. Mr. Vreeden is dead!'"

DeKok feigned astonishment.

"Dead?" he wondered aloud. "But, then, what about the address?"

Grauw resignedly pulled up his shoulders.

"I think she must have found it in one of my desk drawers. As I said, she was always rummaging through other peoples' things."

DeKok spread both hands. He seemed abashed.

"This is all beyond my comprehension." There was genuine despair in his voice. DeKok could be a consummate actor when he wanted to be. "If Marlies van Haesbergen had Mr. Vreeden's address in her hand how could she cling to the belief he was dead?"

Grauw sighed heavily.

"Karin had me called in, because the old woman wouldn't stop," he explained, patiently. "She had no idea how to handle the situation. At Karin's request I confirmed Mr. Vreeden was still on vacation in the Bahamas."

"How did she respond?"

"To my amazement she asked whether he was at the Hotel Out Island Inn in Georgetown." I confirmed the address, as well. She became hostile. She said, in so many words, the address was false and she intended to prove it. She said she had a ticket to Great Exuma. Said she was going to check on Mr. Vreeden herself. She planned to depart soon, maybe tomorrow—I'm not exactly sure."

"And?"

"What?"

"Is that address false?"

Grauw looked at the old inspector with a pitying look.

"I would have expected," he said with scorn, "a man of your experience would be better able to evaluate the conduct of an eccentric old woman." He shook his head. "And, no, the address isn't false." With a frustrated gesture he pushed back the sleeve of his jacket and looked at his watch. "I think," he smirked, "Mr. Vreeden will have just awakened, or is already at breakfast. He continued in a mocking tone. "What's the problem? I'll be happy to give you his phone number in the Bahamas. You can personally inform him of the untimely, er, the passing of Mrs. van Haesbergen. Then you can dispel any doubts you may have by asking after *his* health."

They left the offices of Dredging Works, when the first of the "Thundering Herd" arrived. This was DeKok's manner of referring to the small army of experts, police dignitaries, and omnipresent CSI people who always converged at murder scenes. DeKok's policy was to make himself scarce before they started their work. If CSI or the other experts found anything he could use, fine. Meanwhile he didn't need all the politics or static.

The two inspectors were depressed. No words passed between them. Their encounter with the glib, oily Grauw left them both uneasy. Each ruminated over the events of the last few hours.

They reached the back of the Royal Palace, when DeKok finally broke the silence.

"Did he come on the line at once?"

Vledder shook his head.

"No, first I reached an English speaking man … maybe a desk clerk or switchboard operator. There was a bit of static before he came on the line."

"How did he answer?"

"He sounded normal. 'This is Vreeden,' he said."

"Then what?"

They played this game of questions and answers so often it was a ritual. DeKok already knew some of the answers, but he wanted to set it firmly in both their minds. Repetition, he often said, insures accuracy.

Vledder shrugged.

"I identified myself as an inspector with the Amsterdam Police. I said the old widow of his concierge had been murdered, strangled with a scarf. There was a moment's silence at the other end. It seemed he was deeply shocked by the news. A moment later he returned with, 'How terrible—I hope you will catch the perpetrator quickly.' That's all he said."

"His health is good?"

Vledder grinned.

"I didn't ask. He sounded pretty lively to me."

DeKok nodded his understanding.

"You should have passed on greetings," he said after a while.

"From …"

"Xaveria Breerode. You could have said, for instance, she's been very worried."

Vledder stopped walking.

"By God," he exclaimed, "you're right. I can't believe I forgot about Xaveria. Of course, I should have asked why he didn't, at least, leave a message for her." He paused and resumed walking. He gave DeKok an accusing look. "It's your own fault. You let me make the call. Why didn't you do it yourself?"

The gray sleuth was unabashed.

"My English is not all that good ... over the telephone."

"What's different over the phone?"

DeKok nodded resignedly.

"Then I can't use my hands and feet."

Vledder thought about that for a moment. Then the accusing look disappeared and a twinkle came to his eyes.

"Mr. Vreeden is a Dutchman. He'd have been most comfortable speaking Dutch."

"Whoever answered the phone wasn't."

They continued on in silence, across the Damrak, past the Beehive Department Store toward Old Bridge Alley.

Vledder was clearly deep in thought. Heavy wrinkles furrowed his forehead.

"You know what I don't understand?" he asked suddenly.

"Well?"

"If Mr. Vreeden is alive there's no apparent motive for anyone to kill Marlies."

DeKok grinned broadly.

"Dick Vledder," he mocked, "sometimes you almost convince me that you have a brain in there."

"Go jump in a lake."

12

___

Vledder slowed down.

"Is there anything else you want to do tonight?"

"What time is it?"

Vledder looked at his watch.

"Almost ten o'clock."

They walked on, but at the corner of Warmoes Street, Vledder halted again.

"It's Celine's birthday, today," he said. "And she's in town. I would like to stop by."

"Congratulations."

"Thanks."

DeKok looked worried.

"I don't hear much about your love life, lately."

Vledder grimaced.

"What do you want? Between you and me, my job in crime, and her job with KLM it doesn't leave a lot of time for love."

"How long have you been engaged?"

"Years."

"Marriage plans?"

Vledder was uncomfortable. He scratched the back of his neck.

"I ... eh, I've proposed several times," he said timidly. "But you know what Celine said?"

"How should I?"

"She would stick with me a bit longer. 'Meanwhile,' she said, 'you can stay married to the Warmoes Street and that old geezer.'"

DeKok scowled and pointed an index finger at his chest.

"She was talking about me?"

"None other."

DeKok grinned broadly.

"Well, give her my love and respect," he said cheerily. "And be kind to her. I'm going to put a few lines in the Daily Log and then ..." He did not complete the sentence. The happy grin disappeared. "We'll see each other in the morning."

He turned around and went into the station house.

Jan Kuster looked up from his desk when DeKok entered the lobby. He pointed at the ceiling.

"They're upstairs."

"Who?"

"Buitendam and the judge advocate."

"You told them about the murder at Emperor's Canal?"

"Of course."

"What did they say?"

"They hardly seemed interested."

"Then why are they here?" asked DeKok testily.

Kuster shrugged his shoulders.

"They asked for you. I told them you and Vledder were investigating the reported murder of an old woman. None of them said another word. They passed me and went upstairs. Buitendam turned around at the bottom of the stairs and told me to send you up as soon as you came in."

Commissaris Buitendam sat regally behind his imposing desk. The judge advocate, Mr. Schaap, dressed in an anthracite-gray suit, was seated to the left of the commissaris. DeKok crossed the space to the desk slowly. He had a bad feeling.

"Please, sit down, DeKok." It was a friendly invitation.

Contrary to his usual stubbornness, DeKok took a seat. Meanwhile he studied the two faces before him. The commissaris looked bland and the judge advocate had on his poker face. DeKok always kept in mind the judge advocate was an extremely skillful litigator. No one wanted to spar with him. More than anything DeKok had always disliked the man. By law, the judge advocate is considered to be the lead investigating officer. It was Mr. Schaap's habit, his style, to remain in the background. He seldom, if ever, appeared in public, not even for the most intriguing murder cases. DeKok had little respect for the manner in which the man exercised the duties of his high office. Schaap, he felt, did not show leadership in his policies. He was also easily influenced by pressures from various factions.

Commissaris Buitendam stretched his back.

"The judge advocate and I," he began in his pompous manner, "are extremely pleased to tell you that Mr. Meturovski, the counselor for Dredging Works Vreeden, has rescinded his complaint against you and Vledder *in casu* illegal entry and trespass."

Despite himself, DeKok swallowed hastily.

"In writing?" he asked.

The commissaris shook his head.

"Tonight, by telephone. Written confirmation will be

forthcoming. But we considered the mere revocation of the complaint of sufficient import to inform you at once." Buitendam lifted his chin. "I'd be remiss in not letting you know both the judge advocate and I have repeatedly urged Mr. Meturovski to reconsider what happened in Bergen. We made it clear you and Vledder have admirable, not to say unblemished, records."

DeKok pressed his lips together. His fighting spirit was aroused. He took a deep breath before he spoke.

"In other words, he did it as a favor?"

The judge advocate cleared his throat.

"Look at it as balancing considerations … eh, interests."

"Whose interests?"

"Yours, Vledder's, and Dredging Works Vreeden, who like to maintain an amicable relationship with the judiciary."

DeKok gave Schaap a barely disguised, scornful look.

"Has Mr. Meturovski personally consulted with Mr. Vreeden in this matter?"

The judge advocate put two fingers behind the collar of his shirt as if to give himself air. The question had visibly surprised him.

"I'm sure that has happened. Why do you ask?"

DeKok shook his head.

"I don't believe a word of it."

Mr. Schaap seemed shocked.

"Why should Mr. Meturovski not have consulted with Mr. Vreeden?"

DeKok grinned.

"No consultation took place, because no contact is possible. Mr. Vreeden is dead."

"What?"

DeKok maintained his insolent grin.

"Dead ... dee-ee-aa-dee." He meant to mock them. "For reasons known only to themselves, several people have been active in camouflaging the demise of Mr. Vreeden. There is a conspiracy to make it appear Mr. Vreeden is on vacation in the Bahamas."

Buitendam looked bewildered.

"That cannot be true," he said.

DeKok nodded with emphasis. His impertinent grin had changed to a grim smile.

"But it *is* true. And Mr. Meturovski, the man who so nobly withdrew his complaint, is up to his neck in it."

Mr. Schaap turned red down to his neck. The red color was in stark contrast to his spotless white shirt.

"I presume," he said bitingly, "that you have evidence to support this slanderous accusation?"

DeKok shook his head.

"I regret," he said in a friendly, reconciliatory tone of voice, "we have no hard evidence, not yet. However, until I have evidence, neither Mr. Meturovski nor any of his minions can lead me down the primrose path."

Buitendam's blood pressure climbed precipitously. With a prominent vein throbbing on his head, he stood up from his chair and pointed at the door of the office.

"OUT!!" he roared.

DeKok left.

Jan Kuster looked on as DeKok entered a terse report about the murder at Emperor's Canal in the Daily Log.

"You didn't take long," he said, a question in his voice.

DeKok underlined his entry and looked up.

"We could have taken all day—neither of them has had his first thought," he said venomously.

The watch commander grinned.

"A commissaris of police and a judge advocate?" he said dubiously.

DeKok pushed the log book away and nodded.

"When I say something the gentlemen don't want to hear, they kick me out of the room like a dog. They aren't smart enough to ask questions, let alone listen to answers." He took a deep breath. "If they would just listen, I could explain on what I base my opinions. There could be an exchange of ideas. We could work out a strategy. Their idiotic posturing makes me ..." He did not complete the sentence, but stood up and walked away.

At the counter he stopped and turned around when Kuster called him.

"Are you going home?"

DeKok shook his head.

"No, I'm stopping by at Little Lowee's. I need to get rid of this nasty taste in my mouth.

DeKok ambled through the Red Light District, unhurried. In contrast to the morning and early afternoon, it was very busy. Groups of people crowded in front of the sex cinemas and gaped at inflatable dolls and other sex toys.

The gray sleuth walked by without paying attention. He had on occasion looked into some of the sex-shop windows and had been amazed at the variety with which the phallus had been duplicated. In real life, he was certain, there was not that much variety. Perhaps, he thought, he did not have enough imagination in those matters. It was also why soulless women, inflatable or otherwise, made little impression.

He reached Rear Fort Canal and crossed Old Church Square. Here the street prostitutes crowded along the sidewalks. Some of the older women greeted DeKok and he responded politely. Some of the newer prostitutes tried to entice him, or engage him in conversation. He ignored them. Their sisters in "the life" would set them straight concerning the senior inspector.

Near the corner of Barn Alley, he pushed aside a dark-brown, leather curtain and entered the cozy, dimly lit bar. He'd so often found solace here. Prostitutes taking short breaks occupied most of the tables. Some greeted DeKok, or nodded in his direction. There was no one at the bar. Lowee filled an order for his waitress and turned toward DeKok at the moment the old man hoisted himself onto a stool.

Lowee wiped his hands on his apron and smiled.

"Needa nightcap?" he queried. "And whadda you done wiv da kid?"

"You mean Vledder?"

"Yeah, youse like Siamese."

DeKok smiled.

"It's his fiancée's birthday. He wanted to be with her."

"Dat's awrite. Ya gotta make time for love ..." Lowee did not finish. "Youse know somethin' about Archie, yet?"

DeKok made an apologetic gesture.

"Not much. I'm afraid the boy is mixed up in some dirty business."

"What kinda binis?"

DeKok did not answer at once. He looked a bit wounded.

"Isn't it about time you pour?" he asked pleasantly.

Lowee blushed. He dove under the counter and reached for the special bottle he kept just for DeKok. In no time at all he had poured cognac into two snifters. DeKok watched with interest. Cognac, he felt, was the only drink that could possibly have been created by the gods. The "nectar" that the gods drank on Mt. Olympus must have been cognac.

He lifted one of the glasses and took a careful sip. He savored the taste as the liquid seeped down to his stomach. Then he replaced the glass.

"Have you heard anything about a kidnapping?" he asked casually.

The barkeeper looked surprised.

"A kidnapping?"

"Yes."

"Cmon' Archie ain't messed aroun' widdat?"

DeKok lifted his glass and nodded slowly.

"I have a number of reasons to suspect he was. You see, the guy you sent to see me, Kees Wallen, told me Archie was toting around a big roll of money. He had enough to pay cash for one of Wallen's boats, an old cabin cruiser."

"Whadda 'e want widdat?"

DeKok took another sip.

"A good question—what would he do with it? I found the boat along the Amstel. It had new brass padlocks and a space had been made inside with a cot and a chemical toilet."

The little barkeeper panted.

"To stow somebody?"

"Clearly."

Little Lowee lowered his head. The announcement had touched him deeply.

"Stupid Archie," he sighed. After a while he looked up. "I godda tell ya. Archie ain't gotta brains ta do nuttin like hold somebody fa ransome. Nossir he couldn do it."

DeKok drained his glass.

"It doesn't sound likely, does it. I wonder whether someone used him. Who knows what they promised the boy—money, protection, fast cars, girls." He paused and gave Lowee an intense look. "I don't want you to mention the kidnapping to anybody, for the time being."

"Of course not," promised Lowee, loyally.

"You see," continued DeKok, "we need to find the brains behind this. We need to identify the possible victim, as well."

"If somethin' comes my way?"

DeKok smiled.

"You know how I appreciate your cooperation. You could, for instance, ask around to see who might have been doing some remodeling on a boat."

"Onna boat they was gonna use?"

"Exactly."

"Archie musta done it 'isself. Go take a look at Fat Nellie's place. He done A-one carpentry."

DeKok accepted a second glass of cognac.

"Has Handsome Karl gone to see Fat Nellie?"

Lowee grimaced.

"Handsome Karl and Fat Nellie?"

DeKok nodded.

"He told me he had lived with her for about a year, some time ago. Then I told him to go visit her. She needed a friend."

Little Lowee grinned.

"Karl ain't gonna show 'is face there. He ain't crazy.

Nellie put 'er scissors inn 'is back one time. Ain't nothin' to say she won't do 'im in!"

"What made her stab him?"

"Wadda ya expeck? Karl was tryin' ta strangle 'er wid a scarf."

13

DeKok looked shocked.

"Strangled ... with a scarf?"

"Yep, 'at he brought along 'isself."

"I never knew."

The small barkeeper shook his head nonchalantly.

"Nobody said nuttin'. Why go to da cops aboudit? Karl wore dem scissors inna cab alla way to da doc. He was awrite after coupla days. When he come around, Nell and me, we tole 'im to buzz off for good, geddit?"

DeKok nodded his understanding.

"He took off for The Hague."

Little Lowee frowned.

"Da Hague? Whadda ya mean, Da Hague?"

DeKok waved his hand about.

"He told me he had been picked up by the police in The Hague for a break-in in a villa. Apparently he did a few months in jail there."

Lowee looked pensive and shook his head.

"You an' da kid better check widdacops inna Hague. Karl gots pals in high places—bin caretakin' for some rich buzzard. Da rich guy hadda house and a lotta land in Ireland. Karl was lookin' out for it."

DeKok could not resist a laugh.

"Karl guarding other peoples' property. That, my

friend, is like a lion herding zebras," he snickered.

Lowee laughed, too.

"But it musta been a bust, or 'e wouldna come back so soon."

"Is he still around?"

Lowee shrugged.

"I ain't seen hide or hair—ain't heard nuttin'."

"How did you get in contact with Karl?"

"Years ago, or now?"

"When you sent him to me."

Lowee looked at the snifters, noticed they were empty, and poured generous measures again.

"Karl come in here, sudden like an' he wanna know have I seen Archie. So I tells Karl, Archie gone widdout a trace. I tole him you was on da case an' you hadna gon nowheres. Then Karl sounds sorta scared. He says Archie bin spillin' about a stiff an' where to plant it."

DeKok nodded.

"That's what he told me. That's why you sent him to me?"

"Yessir."

DeKok sipped his cognac in silence. Then he stared into the glass for a long time. Lowee also seemed to be lost in thought. He absent-mindedly filled some orders for the waitress.

Finally DeKok broke the silence.

"That rich, eh, guy in Ireland? Do you have a name?"

Little Lowee spread his hands.

"No idear."

"Can you find out?"

"Maybe, maybe not. I gotta think who tol' me about Karl and Ireland." He wiped the top of the bar. "Why don't you ax Karl?"

"I don't know where to find him."

"I'll put out a coupla feelers."

DeKok drank the rest of his drink in one swallow and slipped off the stool. As he stood on the floor he spoke again.

"While you're asking around, ask Tattoo Peter and his cronies whether they've put a sort of knight's sword in red and blue on somebody's arm or leg."

Lowee looked scandalized.

"Hey. You da dick!"

DeKok did not answer. He waved goodbye and left.

Early, at least an hour before he expected Vledder, DeKok was at his desk. He wanted to organize his thoughts. He placed a legal pad in front of him on the desk. It was a gesture of bravura. Since Marlies van Haesbergen appeared in the detective room he'd felt drawn into a vortex. There had been, he thought, strange developments, contradictory developments.

The decision to accept Marlies' account as accurate was a stretch. Ever since he'd doubted himself. What had happened to Vreeden? Was he still alive or dead?

The casual attitude of the unpleasant Mr. Grauw, Vreeden's co-director, was surprising. More surprising was his offer of Mr. Vreeden's phone number in the Bahamas. Vledder had reached a man who said he was Vreeden. If that were the case, why would anyone want to kill Marlies? Did she become a threat because she let it be known she intended to go there? Who would be threatened by her appearance there? In any event how would Vreeden have gotten into the Bahamas without his passport? Or was the man in the Bahamas an impostor? If so, who was he? Does Grauw know?

Something else plagued DeKok. Even the wealthy, powerful Mr. Vreeden was only mortal. If he had exchanged the temporal for the eternal, why hide it? Even if he died from some dread disease would it be reason to keep the police out of it? On the other hand, if Paul Vreeden was murdered, the killer would wish to get rid of the corpse. Could he conclude the murderer was eliminating evidence?

"DeKok!"

The startled old man looked up and saw the laughing face of Vledder.

"What's going on?" he asked, confused and irritated.

"You're getting old."

"Now tell me something I don't know."

"You were talking to yourself."

DeKok smiled self-consciously.

"I was thinking. I just didn't realize I was thinking out loud."

Vledder pointed at the legal pad.

"What do you want with that?"

"I'm putting my thoughts on paper."

Vledder grinned.

"I never knew you had such clean thoughts, the paper is still pristine."

DeKok tore off the first, blank sheet, crumpled it, and tossed it in the wastebasket. He slid the note pad into a drawer.

"You're pretty sharp this morning," he said. "The birthday party must have been a success."

He stood up and walked over to where he kept his coat and hat.

Vledder followed.

"Are we off already?"

"Yes."

"Where to?"

"Amersfoort. I want to ask Xaveria Breerode if she wants to make a phone call for us."

On Precious Lady Square in Amersfoort stands Precious Lady Church. The church is an imposing structure, nearly three hundred feet tall. Vledder parked the police VW and turned off the ignition. He looked at the surroundings.

"Does she live here?"

DeKok pointed.

"We have a bit farther to go. She's on Precious Lady Street, just past the Lamme Goetsack."

Vledder laughed.

"Whatever is the *Lamme Goetsack*?"

"A kind of bistro, actually, very nice. It is named after the rotund friend of Tijil Uilenspiegel. You may recall Tijil Uilenspiegel's Merry Pranks, by Richard Strauss. Uilenspiegel was a renowned trickster in sixteenth century Flanders. The bistro is one of the few places Xaveria and Paul Vreeden frequented.

"You're well informed."

"The study of history is never a waste. You know, people who do not understand their history are doomed to repeat it."

"Spare me the lecture. I meant, how do you know about Xaveria and the restaurant?"

"Last night, rather late, I called the Amersfoort police."

Vledder looked up.

"Did they know about Xaveria Breerode?"

DeKok nodded.

"She has no criminal background, if that's what you mean. The watch commander, though, recalled her name. It seems a former colleague of his, a private detective, was very interested in her."

"Who was his client?"

"Our Amersfoort colleague also wanted to know."

"And?"

"It was a notary."

Vledder wrinkled his nose.

"A notary ... a lawyer? What kind of lawyer?"

"That's something the private detective did not reveal."

"When would a notary require the services of a private eye?"

"Usually the private detective would act as a representative, for example, assisting a wealthy individual who is contemplating a will or—"

Vledder interrupted enthusiastically.

"One who wants to check on the character and activities of, say, a beneficiary?"

DeKok nodded. Vledder remained silent. Suddenly he banged the steering wheel with his fist.

"No, it would be too coincidental," he exclaimed.

"What are you thinking?" demanded DeKok.

"Well," said Vledder, hesitantly, "what if Vreeden was the one who had Meturovski check her out. As in-house counsel, Meturovski would be both a solicitor and a notary. He would handle wills as a matter of course."

That was as far as he got. DeKok suddenly pushed his

head down below the level of the dashboard.

"Quiet," he hissed, "I don't want him to see us."

"Who?"

"Gerard Grauw. He just came out of Precious Lady Street with a briefcase in his hand."

Xaveria Breerode, dressed in a diaphanous lace dressing gown, looked at the inspectors with large eyes.

"A phone call? For this you came all the way from Amsterdam to Amersfoort?" She smiled her disbelief. "And whom do you want me to call?"

DeKok did not take his eyes off her face.

"Paul Vreeden," he said evenly.

Her face lit up.

"You know where he is?"

DeKok did not answer. He pulled a piece of paper out of the breast pocket of his jacket. He gave it to her.

"This is the telephone number of a Hotel Out Island Inn. It's near the beach, in Georgetown, in the Bahamas."

"And Paul is there?"

DeKok shook his head, no.

"We only suspect he's there." He pointed at Vledder, "My colleague called the number yesterday and talked to a man who identified himself as Mr. Vreeden. The man spoke in a candid, relaxed manner." He smiled a bashful smile. "However we do not know Mr. Vreeden's voice. We haven't sufficient, ahem, unusual details or intimacies to trip up an imposter."

Xaveria looked furious.

"But I do know … unusual details and intimacies? Is that it?"

DeKok spread his hands.

"We assume so, yes, but please do not mistake our intentions. We also assume the phone call is as important to you as it may be to us. I take it you are still very much concerned about Mr. Vreeden?"

Her beautiful almond eyes narrowed.

"Of course I am."

DeKok gave her his most winning smile.

"Then ... why don't you call him?"

She looked from DeKok to Vledder and back again.

"And you want to be present?"

DeKok nodded emphatically.

"You must understand we are also concerned."

Xaveria sighed deeply. She pushed a hassock over and took a bizarre looking telephone from a fragile little table. The phone was alight with green onyx. She placed the instrument on her knees and started to dial.

DeKok looked around the room. The room was decorated in a subtle, distinctly Asian style, with lamps on the walls and Chinese screens. He changed his position. Because of an enormous mirror he could look into the bedroom and at the unmade bed. Although he saw no evidence of it, he wondered if Gerard Grauw had spent the night in the bed.

He had the feeling of being sucked again into a vortex. His search for the missing managing director propelled him into a muddy whirlpool of lechery and crime. It was a paralyzing feeling.

Xaveria's conversation was like background noise. Although he was right next to her, she seemed far away. The sound passed by him like the rustling of the wind in the trees. Only after she had finished and hung up the receiver, did he look at her. She was suddenly very pale, he noticed. She had dark circles under her eyes, and drops of perspiration beaded her forehead.

"Mr. Vreeden," she said hoarsely, "is no longer in the hotel. A few hours ago he left for an undetermined destination and left no forwarding address."

DeKok remained emotionless.

"This is what I feared," he said softly. "We will have to send a photo of Mr. Vreeden to the police in Georgetown. Just to be sure. They can show it to the hotel personnel. Do you have a picture we may borrow?"

Xaveria slumped down. She barely responded, as though she had become a timid little bird.

DeKok leaned over, took the telephone from her lap, and replaced it on the table. Then he pulled a second hassock closer and sat down across from her.

"Now you know how very concerned we are. Mr. Vreeden's departure appeared precipitous." His voice sounded friendly and solicitous. "We're looking for an explanation."

Xaveria nodded submissively.

"Of course."

"Was Mr. Vreeden in good health?"

"How do you mean?"

"Did he suffer from some kind of malady—fears, anxieties, depression—did he see a doctor?"

For a moment the woman closed her eyes.

"Paul sometimes had chest pains. Last year he had a mild heart attack. The doctor advised him to take it easier. Paul had a regimen of diet and exercise for weight loss and to lower his blood pressure. He had hypertension. Dr. Haanstra in Amsterdam is his physician and prescribes for him."

"Did he not have a doctor in Bergen?"

She shook her head.

"He didn't want to bother. He has a phone number for emergencies, but it was easier to see the doctor in Amsterdam. He could consult him during office hours."

"And he did?"

"Certainly."

DeKok stared in front of him thoughtfully. Suddenly a spark—he flashed back to the previous night at Little Lowee's.

"Have you ever been to Ireland?" he asked.

Xaveria looked surprised.

"At Thundering Heights?"

DeKok bit his lower lip. The question had been an impulse. The answer baffled him. For a moment his heart seemed to skip a beat. He regained his poise.

"Is that the name of the property?" he asked casually.

Xaveria nodded.

"It's a bit raw and wild and there are a lot of storms. It's near the coast in the south of Ireland. Paul bought it last spring, for us. He was so looking forward to lightening his workload at the firm." Her face fell. "It seems an unreachable dream for the time being. The inside of the mansion has been sadly neglected. There's a lot of work to be done."

DeKok slowly rubbed the bridge of his nose with his little finger. He was tense. He did not completely succeed in controlling the shaking of his hand.

"Is the estate now deserted?"

"Paul hired a caretaker."

"Do you know his name?"

"Koperman."

The gray sleuth sighed and beamed. For the first time during this strange investigation, he felt a slight triumph.

Vledder looked aside. The sparkle in his partner's eyes made him wonder.

"Koperman," repeated Vledder, not understanding.

DeKok grinned.

"That's Handsome Karl's surname."

14

From the parking lot on Precious Lady Square, the inspectors drove toward the highway. They passed a number of beautifully preserved canals in the picturesque inner city of Amersfoort. Vledder was behind the wheel as usual, but looking contrite. He felt left out. The entire search for Vreeden seemed to have passed him by. With an angry look he glanced at his partner.

"Impossible," he growled. "Karl was in jail. He told us so, himself."

DeKok nodded.

"Did you check it out?"

"No, why should I?"

"Exactly, you had no pressing reason to do so. As far as we are concerned he's no more than a casual witness. Given his reputation it seemed as plausible to me as it did to you. But last night I also phoned The Hague."

"You've been busy ... what made you call The Hague?"

Silently DeKok laughed at Vledder's defensiveness.

"You don't have to be so hard on yourself," he said mildly. "If anything, I'd have to share the blame. We were equally taken aback by the news of Karl's engagement as the caretaker in Ireland." He pushed himself upright in his seat. "While you were at your party I had a couple of enlightening experiences."

"Such as?"

DeKok smirked.

"Our very own commissaris, accompanied by Judge Advocate Schaap, was waiting for me at the station. They wished to personally acquaint me with the happy tiding that Mr. Meturovski had withdrawn his complaint against us."

"What?"

"Yes. You can stop losing sleep."

Vledder snorted.

"I'm sleeping fine," he growled.

DeKok smirked again.

"Despite the happy announcement, it was not a pleasant conversation. The two esteemed gentlemen wanted to take credit for the withdrawal of the complaint. After all hadn't they gone to bat for us, telling Mr. Meturovski we are such good boys? Suddenly the depth of the manure became too much for me."

A smile broke out on Vledder's morose face.

"They excused you forthwith."

"Ah but there is more. To revive my sagging spirits, I paid a call on Little Lowee."

"Oh, it was Lowee who told you about the estate in Ireland and Handsome Karl."

DeKok momentarily closed his eyes.

"Just let me think a moment," he said. "I want to be sure you get the complete story. I asked if Karl had gone to see Fat Nellie. You remember, I told him Nellie could use a friend. Well, Lowee told me it would be stupid for Karl to go to Nell. The last time they saw each other she placed a pair of scissors in his back, sharp end first."

"Why?"

"Because Handsome Karl was displaying his utter devotion by strangling her with a scarf."

Vledder's eyes widened.

"The plot thickens," he exclaimed, "with a scarf, no less."

"He had brought it along for the very purpose," added DeKok.

"Then what?"

"After a few days' recovery, Karl was back on his feet. Fat Nellie and Little Lowee made sure he understood henceforth he was *persona no grata* in the fair city of Amsterdam. That is why Handsome Karl wound up in The Hague," he concluded.

Vledder grinned.

"That's why he concocted the story of his arrest in The Hague."

"Little Lowee looked at me in utter disbelief when I told him about Karl and The Hague. He set me straight. According to him, Karl had found a job in Ireland, babysitting some rich guy's house."

"Aha. Then you connected the dots and came up with Vreeden as the possible employer. *That's* why you asked Xaveria if she'd ever been in Ireland." He patted DeKok on the shoulder. "Well done."

"Thank you."

"Excuse me for asking, what are we supposed to do with the glut of information?"

"Nothing."

"But," sputtered Vledder, "I thought you were very pleased to have the name Koperman."

"As far as it goes, yes, I am. For now, though, I can't put it to use. It merely proves Handsome Karl knew

Mr. Vreeden. You see, Karl comes in two distinct but inseparable personas. He is handsome on the surface, but crooked down deep. Vreeden's wealth must have started him thinking. Karl may not be gullible or slow, but he's no criminal mastermind."

"What do you mean by that?"

"Something tells me these events, particularly surrounding Vreeden's disappearance, are being orchestrated. Someone in the background is the brains behind it."

"I see."

"Yes, and now I'll take a little nap. It was a short night. Wake me when we get back to Amsterdam."

He slid down in the seat and pulled his hat over his eyes.

When they reached the city, Vledder nudged him. DeKok woke up and looked around.

"Drop me off on Emperor's Canal," he said.

"You're not going back to the station?"

"No, you are. When you get there, call Kruger and tell him to look for Karl's prints. They will be in his collection. It would be nice if we could find a match in the apartment of Marlies."

"And you?"

"I'm going to have a little chat with Dr. Haanstra, Paul Vreeden's chest man."

DeKok climbed the bluestone steps of the imposing stoop. He looked at the brass plate next to the green, lacquered door. In deeply engraved black letters it read: *j. e. haanstra, m. d. consultations from 10:00 until 12:00.* From where he stood he could just see a church clock. It was fifteen minutes before noon. He pushed open the heavy door and followed an arrow to the waiting room. The only people in the room were two women. DeKok nodded a greeting and sat down in a rattan chair. He picked up an old magazine and held it before his face.

As the women discussed their various ailments in embarrassing detail, DeKok tried to close his ears. A buzzer went and one woman disappeared into the consulting room. DeKok felt the remaining woman desperately trying to make eye contact. DeKok felt in no way inclined to get involved with her digestive tract. He hid behind his magazine. The buzzer went off again and DeKok found himself alone. He replaced the magazine and waited patiently.

After about twenty minutes, the consulting room door opened. DeKok saw a tall, young man in a sparkling white coat. DeKok estimated him to be about thirty years old. His hair was blond and there was the beginning of a beard on his cheeks.

"Are you the last one?" he asked.

DeKok looked around the room.

"Nobody came in after I did."

"Please step this way," said the young man.

The inspector followed him into the consulting room with his hat in his hand.

"You're not a patient of mine?"

"No."

"What is your name?"

DeKok … with a kay-oh-kay. In full, Jurriaan DeKok, Jurre to my friends," he added. Actually nobody, except his wife, ever called him anything else but "DeKok."

The young doctor sat down behind his desk and invited DeKok to take the seat opposite. The doctor took a blank, pre-printed card and started to make entries.

"What are your complaints?"

"A vanished managing director."

The doctor looked up in surprise.

"What did you say?"

DeKok smiled faintly.

"A vanished managing director," he repeated in a friendly voice. "One Paul Vreeden."

The gold fountain pen slipped from the doctor's fingers and made a blot on the new card.

"Mr. Vreeden?"

DeKok nodded.

"You are Dr. Haanstra?"

"Certainly—yes, I am."

DeKok smiled a disarming smile.

"And Mr. Vreeden *was* your patient?" He emphasized the word "was" in the hope of a reaction from the doctor. There was none.

"Yes, that is to say, he has consulted me from time to time."

"Complaints?"

Surprisingly the young physician responded with little hesitation. "Mr. Vreeden has a weak heart and needs to schedule an operation. His general health is not good for a man his age—his blood pressure is much too high."

"Apparently you know about his disappearance?"

It was as if the young doctor suddenly came out of anesthesia.

"Who are you?" he asked suddenly, sharply.

DeKok pointed at the card on the desk.

"You already have my name. I'm a police inspector, attached to Warmoes Street Station, here in Amsterdam."

He made a rueful gesture. "I wanted to tell you right away, but you were so efficient, so professional, I—"

Doctor Haanstra interrupted vehemently.

"You should have identified yourself immediately," he stormed. "That is your obligation. You tricked me into revealing confidential information about my patient."

DeKok shrugged.

"I asked if you knew about his disappearance. You haven't answered."

Haanstra shook his head.

"No, I was not aware. As far as I knew Mr. Vreeden was on vacation in the Bahamas."

"Did Mr. Vreeden tell you he was going on vacation, say, in connection with medicines he was taking?"

"Yes, yes," hesitated the doctor. "He told me. In fact he was acting on my advice. I felt it would be beneficial for his total well being to get away from work for a while."

"Why the Bahamas?"

The doctor was getting agitated.

"It was his call," he said, testily. "He could have gone to Volendam, as far as I was concerned." He paused and a suspicious look came into his blue eyes. "Who says Mr. Vreeden has disappeared?"

DeKok tapped his chest.

"I do."

The doctor's anger escalated.

"You?" he mocked. "Who are you to take up my time because you have decided Mr. Vreeden has disappeared?"

The cynical tone made no impression on the old sleuth. He was convinced the young doctor knew more than he revealed. He looked around the room. On the desk he noticed a brown chest with drawers. The tops of cards protruded from some drawers. Plastic dividers separated the cards alphabetically. It was obviously the doctor's patient file. There were only a few cards under "V."

He left the doctor's question unanswered and pointed to the incomplete card under the doctor's hand.

"Do you fill out a card like that for all your patients?"

"Certainly."

"Also for Mr. Vreeden?"

Dr. Haanstra paled. His hand moved to the card file, but DeKok was faster. With one hand he pushed the box out of the reach of the doctor and with the other hand he lifted the cards under "V" out from behind the divider. One by one the cards went through his hands. When the last card had been replaced on the desk, he looked up. With a threatening look on his face he stood up.

"Dr. Haanstra, there is no card here for Mr. Vreeden."

15

DeKok walked back to Warmoes Street from Emperor's Canal. He was not happy. The conversation with the young doctor had ended with a vague, unsatisfactory, explanation as to why Paul Vreeden's patient card was missing. It was food for thought. DeKok also thought Dr. Haanstra knew more. Once again DeKok had more questions than answers. Was the doctor's reticence indicative of his involvement in the conspiracy? What was his connection to all of this?

It started to rain, a penetrating, miserable drizzle. It gave a shine to the streets. DeKok raised the collar of his coat and pushed his little hat farther down. He surveyed his surroundings. Amsterdam was at its most beautiful in the rain, he mused. Ancient facades mirrored themselves in the glistening asphalt. Amsterdam sparkled.

As he walked his mood lightened a bit. It could have been the depressing weather. DeKok reveled in what some people found dreary. He went through Palace Street to reach Dam Square. The pigeons seemed to enjoy the rain, too. They flew around, hoping for a handout.

He stopped at a deserted, wet bench. It seemed an age since he had sat here. It was the day he spotted Marlies van Haesbergen and followed her. The day she bought the tickets from the travel agency. An eternity of just two days had passed.

He caught himself going over her death and whether he could have done more to prevent it. He stopped short of agonizing. His old mother had often said, "Man derides, but God decides." DeKok's work gave him a more complicated view. Too many people, he knew, refused to await God's decisions. Rather they took it upon themselves to make life and death decisions. These, he reflected, were the kind of people involved in this macabre dance. What was it they wanted? He desperately wanted to pinpoint a motive.

He tried to picture the elusive Mr. Vreeden. Paul Vreeden's passport photo helped little. It did reveal the face of a forceful man, a man who knew what he wanted. Xaveria Breerode had given an eloquent description of a man whose high energy level belied his stress level. His character she described as old fashioned, open, and uncomplicated. He distributed 1,000 Euro notes like candy in high-stakes gambles for multi-million dollar contracts. Did Paul Vreeden's habit of spreading cash around provide someone a motive?

Suddenly DeKok's sunny nature broke through. A light came on in the dark recesses of his brain. For a moment he imagined that a sunbeam had penetrated the thick, gray clouds above and hit him in the neck. He licked a raindrop from his upper lip and walked on with a broad grin on his face.

Vledder shook his head.

"Ben Kruger could not do anything with Handsome Karl's prints. The only fingerprints in the apartment were those of the occupant and her niece, plus a few partials. There were traces of gloves."

DeKok received the news passively as he sank down in his chair.

"What did you do with the scarf?"

"I put it in a plastic bag," he said as he opened a drawer in his desk. "I handled it with tweezers." He produced the bag from the drawer. "I haven't sent it to the lab because I was thinking we could use it to set a trap."

"What sort of trap?"

"I thought we could use a canine. We let the dog sniff Karl. Then we let the dog sniff about a dozen scarves. One of them will be this scarf. If Karl handled the scarf, the dog will pick it out."

DeKok looked dubious.

"I don't know about that. If you let the dog sniff you, wouldn't the dog pick out the scarf *you* handled? Wouldn't the dog automatically match the last smell it was exposed to? No, I don't have much faith in it, other than as a last resort." He raised a finger in the air. "Even if the dog *were* to identify Karl, a jury might find it interesting, but the courts would not count it as evidence."

Vledder's shoulders drooped.

"So you have a better idea of how to catch him? Or do we wait for the next murder victim, and hope Karl makes a mistake?" He sounded bitter.

DeKok stood up and leaned over his young colleague.

"Do you know who the next victim is?" he asked.

Vledder lowered his head.

"It's all so disheartening," he sighed. "I can't figure out what it's all about." He looked up. "Did the doctor know anything?"

"Yes," said DeKok slowly, "he knew a lot more than he told me."

"Haanstra?"

"Yes."

"What could he know?"

DeKok did not answer. He had noticed a shadow behind the frosted glass inset of the door. Then there was a knock on the door.

"Come in," yelled DeKok, across the empty room.

It took a few seconds. The door swung open. A short, corpulent man appeared in the opening. He wore a rumpled, brown suit. The rain had plastered his receding hair to his skull. His tanned face was round and puffy with deep circles under slightly bulging eyes.

DeKok beckoned. The man approached, breathing heavily.

"Are you Inspector DeKok?"

"Indeed."

The man fished a large red handkerchief from a pocket and wiped the sweat and rain off his forehead.

"I would like to speak to you."

DeKok pointed at the chair near his desk.

"Please have a seat."

The man hesitated, looked around the room and at Vledder.

"Privately."

DeKok shook his head.

"This is my colleague, Vledder. He hears, sees, and does not speak."

The man sat down, obviously disappointed.

"My information is of a confidential nature, I would rather have no—"

"Witnesses?"

"No, no, that's not what I mean," protested the man.

"I just don't want anything to leak out. Nobody knows I'm here."

"You prefer to remain anonymous?"

"That's not necessary." The man shook his head. "I don't mind you knowing who I am. My name is Middelkoop, Henri Middelkoop. I'm one of the directors of Dredging Works Vreeden at Emperor's Canal."

DeKok took a chair across from his visitor, his back to Vledder. He gestured breezily.

"It looks as though you just returned from the Bahamas."

Middelkoop's face froze.

"No, no, you're mistaken. Mr. Vreeden is in the Bahamas. I just returned from the south of France."

"I beg your pardon," said DeKok, smiling mildly.

Middelkoop again gripped his handkerchief and moved in his chair.

"There have been," he began diffidently, "some strange developments in my office during my absence. I refer, in particular, to the death of Mrs. van Haesbergen. It has affected me deeply."

"To be sure, however, you have not mentioned the disappearance of Mr. Vreeden," asked DeKok evenly. Behind him he heard the soft clicking of Vledder's keyboard.

Henri Middelkoop worried his necktie with stubby, fat fingers. He was visibly nervous.

"I understand you have some theories concerning that?"

"What is it you understand?"

"You think Mr. Vreeden is deceased."

"Who told you that?"

"Mr. Schaap."

DeKok was genuinely surprised and showed it.

"Our Mr. Schaap, the judge advocate?"

"Yes," nodded Middelkoop. "I've known Mr. Schaap for some time. I contacted him in connection with the brutal murder of Mrs. van Haesbergen. I insist this horrible crime be solved."

DeKok tried hard to suppress his anger.

"And Mr. Schaap told you I was handling the case. In passing he shared my obsession with the crazy theory Mr. Vreeden also had passed away." The sarcasm dripped off his every word.

Middelkoop took a deep breath.

"Yes, that is about the way it went." He added, "Grauw also spoke with me. He said you rejected his assurances Mr. Vreeden was on vacation. He said you absolutely did not believe it."

DeKok nodded emphatically.

"Mr. Grauw understood perfectly."

Middelkoop leaned closer.

"Inspector," he almost whispered, "reliable sources inform me you're a very experienced police officer with a distinguished record of service. You seem unlikely to jump to irresponsible conclusions. Would you be able to share with me the basis of your doubts?"

DeKok leered at the rotund director. Middelkoop's tone was an affront and irked him.

DeKok responded slowly, and as evenly as he could. "It would be ill-advised for me to go any further."

Middelkoop made a submissive gesture.

"I'm a director of a large firm. I have responsibilities. Therefore I want to know what happens around me. Surely, you can understand that?"

"I understand completely," said DeKok. "However as

long as my investigations are in progress, I don't issue bulletins, progress reports, or information."

Middelkoop took out his handkerchief again and acted like a desperate man.

"But you can surely take *me* into your confidence," he beseeched. "Perhaps we could help each other. I've been with the firm for more than twenty-five years. Perhaps I could help with the investigation."

DeKok looked impassively at the man. He wondered whether Middelkoop was sincere, or just a very good actor. "Oh, what tangled webs we weave, when first we practice to deceive," he quoted to himself.

"And how long has Mr. Grauw been a director?"

"About three years."

"Did he also come up through the ranks?"

Middelkoop shook his head.

"No, Mr. Vreeden introduced him. He felt Grauw would infuse some fresh blood."

"Was there a need—was the business in a slump?"

"No, I should say not. We continue to fill contracts worldwide."

DeKok smiled mischievously.

"In other words Mr. Vreeden generates business."

"Yes, of course. Paul has numerous contacts, especially in the Near East."

"Who would benefit from his death?"

Middelkoop looked confused.

"Yes, who would profit from his death?"

The director's bulging eyes protruded even more.

"Xaveria," he swallowed. "Xaveria Breerode inherits his entire fortune."

16

———————

Middelkoop's answer was predictable. DeKok had already surmised money played an important role in the affair. For several seconds he merely stared at the sweating director. Meanwhile his brain worked at full capacity.

"So Xaveria Breerode is the sole beneficiary under Mr. Vreeden's will," he said in a detached way. "She inherits everything?" The question was intended to gain time.

"Yes."

"How do you know this?"

"Mr. Grauw and I received a copy of the will from the notary."

"Who is Mr. Vreeden's notary?"

"The name is Sugtelen."

"When, exactly, did the notary provide the copy to the two of you?"

"It was about a month ago."

"And before that time Mr. Vreeden gave no indication of his intent?"

Middelkoop shook his head.

"The subject never arose. The will came as a thunder-clap on a clear day. We never saw it coming."

"What was your expectation?"

Middelkoop did not answer. He appeared not to have

heard DeKok's question. He picked at the lapels of his jacket nervously. There was a pained look on his face.

DeKok leaned forward.

"What did the two of you expect?" he repeated.

Middelkoop swallowed.

"I believed Mr. Vreeden would, at the very least, guarantee the continued survival of the firm."

"This was not the case?"

"There are no specific provisions for the company in the will. Xaveria Breerode is both executrix and sole, universal, beneficiary. Although the firm carries his name it is not included as a beneficiary. In fact the only mention of it is as part of the list of assets to be inherited. There is some wording to the effect, 'including, but not limited to the assets listed herein.' The instrument lists some of the major assets, such as 'house with contents' and 'all shares.' Miss Breerode can do whatever she wishes with the stock. If she decides to put the shares on the market after his death, it will be catastrophic for the firm."

"And would she do that?"

"I don't know."

"Do you know her?"

"No."

"Does Mr. Grauw know her?"

Middelkoop took a deep breath.

"I'm not interested in Grauw's private life."

DeKok shook his head in disapproval.

"But the private behavior of Mr. Grauw certainly interests me," he said sharply. "Does Mr. Grauw or does he not know Xaveria Breerode?"

Middelkoop again sought refuge with his large handkerchief. Wiping his forehead and neck. DeKok's very pointed questioning made him uneasy. He tried in vain to avoid DeKok's eyes.

"I presume so," he said finally, softly.

"Why?"

Middelkoop moved uneasily in his chair, twisting the crumpled handkerchief.

"Eh, when Grauw was reading the copy of Vreeden's will, he suddenly threw it down. He screamed angrily, 'That Bitch.'"

"He referred to her as a bitch?"

"Yes."

DeKok rubbed the bridge of his nose with his little finger.

"Bitch—was that a character analysis?"

"Yes, you could say so. He was basing the epithet on ... personal experience."

DeKok remained silent for a long time. He took pity on the corpulent, sweating man. He wanted him to relax, regain his composure. When he finally spoke his voice was less harsh. There was even a little smile around his lips.

"How was your vacation in the south of France?" he asked. "Did you enjoy it?"

"Excellent, I had a very good time."

This time DeKok smirked maliciously.

"I don't know whether you will be due more vacation time this year, but I can recommend an excellent hotel—Hotel Out Island Inn ... in Georgetown on Grand Exuma."

Middelkoop left, breathing deeply and still sweating profusely. DeKok turned his chair around and looked at Vledder.

"You got it all?" he asked.

"Yes," said Vledder. "But I don't understand why you recommended that hotel in the Bahamas to him."

"Don't worry," DeKok said. Under his breath he muttered, "Our Mr. Henri Middelkoop understood me."

"There's something else."

"What?"

"Why did Grauw visit *that bitch* this morning?"

DeKok stood up. Laughingly he placed a hand on Vledder's shoulder.

"You're a phenomenon. You manage to switch from moments of total darkness to brilliant insight in the blink of an eye."

Vledder's face revealed his irritation. He knew DeKok was having fun at his expense.

"You wanted to make sure Middelkoop understood," he said with great irritation, "you don't believe, for a moment, he vacationed in the south of France."

DeKok was genuinely pleased.

"Excellent," he said with admiration in his voice. "Forgive my remark about moments of darkness."

Vledder raised his eyebrows, but he did not smile.

"Darkness, light, whatever," he snapped. "What I got out of it is this: Middelkoop is up to his buggy eyes in this nasty business."

DeKok did not answer, but walked over to get his coat and hat. Vledder followed hastily.

"Where are you going?"

"To Gentleman's Canal," DeKok tossed over his shoulder. "I want a word with Mr. Vreeden's notary, Sugtelen. I want to know why …" He could not finish the sentence. With a sigh he placed his hat on the peg. One of the detectives near the door was directing a visitor in his direction. When he recognized her, the expression on DeKok's face changed to one of warm welcome. He walked toward the visitor.

"Fat Nellie," he said, "come, sit down."

He led her to his desk and seated her with old-world elegance.

"You chanced it after all?" he asked.

"What?" she asked, still a bit flustered.

"You've come to the station. I thought you didn't like the idea of coming here."

"Nobody needs these idlers around here gossiping. They see you here, they assume you're a snitch. Lowee couldn't find anybody to fill in for him, otherwise I wouldn't be here."

"Understandable," said DeKok soothingly. "Thank you for coming."

Nell blushed and mumbled something inaudible.

"So, Lowee asked you to stop by?" asked DeKok brightly, trying to put her at ease.

"Yes."

"You have news?"

Nell leaned forward. Her heavy bosom rested on the edge of the desk. Her face was sad; her tone, fearful.

"DeKok," she pleaded, "do you know anything about my Archie?"

DeKok lowered his head in commiseration. He sighed and looked at her with pity in his eyes.

"Not yet, Nell—it has been slow going," he said hoarsely. "It doesn't look good."

"You mean?"

"We should have heard from him some time ago."

Her eyes filled with tears.

"You don't think Archie—"

DeKok did not let her finish. He nodded slowly.

"We want to know what happened to the boy, too. We'll keep working on it, as long as we can. I promise. But I tell you honestly, at the moment I have no idea where to look."

Fat Nellie wiped her eyes with the back of her hand. The tears had destroyed her makeup. Suddenly there was a hard look in her eyes. Her lips formed a narrow line.

"If that piece of garbage had a hand in it," she hissed, "if he's dared to lay a finger on my boy, I'll kill him. I swear, DeKok. If you catch him, I need five minutes alone. Otherwise some bleeding heart judge will give him a couple of months in jail and a slap on the wrist."

DeKok let her get it out of her system.

"Who are you talking about, Nell?"

She snorted her disdain.

"Handsome Karl."

DeKok was confused.

"How do you figure Karl has anything to do with Archie's disappearance?"

"DeKok, he does. He is Buck Jones."

"What?"

Fat Nellie nodded, a grim look on her face.

"He's the older guy Archie has been hanging around with. I told you he looked familiar."

DeKok reacted sharply.

"How can you be certain?"

She made a movement with her head in the direction of the window.

"Lowee has been to see Tattoo Peter."

DeKok closed his eyes for a moment.

"The tattooed sword," he groaned.

Nell's bosom swayed dangerously.

"Handsome Karl took advantage of Archie by posing as someone he was not."

DeKok took a grieving and distressed Fat Nellie to the watch commander. He arranged to have a police car take her home. When he returned to the detective room, Vledder gaped at him with open mouth.

"You know what this means, DeKok," he blurted out. "Handsome Karl is our mystery guy."

"You are surprised?"

"Then Handsome Karl is also involved with the planned kidnapping."

DeKok nodded agreement.

"You're absolutely right. Based on what Nell told us, we can be sure that Karl was aware of Archie's every move. Archie was rather submissive, because of his disability or his nature. Karl appears to have been more a spiritual leader than merely an older role model. He was able to maneuver Archie into everything. Karl got him to buy the boat, remodel it to include the hiding place."

Vledder bit his lower lip.

"Would Handsome Karl be the brains you felt were behind the kidnap plans?" There was disbelief in his voice. "I've only seen him once, but he seemed more brawn than brain." He sniggered. "I also don't get the 'handsome' in *Handsome* Karl. I've seen no handsome qualities in that rough face."

DeKok smiled.

"His mother was an old-fashioned brothel keeper. That

is, she kept a bar. She provided rooms upstairs for the girls. I remember her well. She had a house on Rear Fort Canal, near Old Acquaintance Alley. The ground floor was the bar. Her living quarters were upstairs, where she kept the girls. Her real name was Mathilde Koperman, but everyone called her Polish Mappie. Why, I don't know. She had children by a number of men. Sometimes she was married, mostly not. As far as Mappie was concerned, there was only one child, her little Karl. She absolutely adored him, attended to his every whim. Although the boy was as ugly as the night, she always called him 'my handsome boy.'"

Vledder understood.

"So it was, he became known in the neighborhood as Handsome Karl."

"Exactly. Maybe it was the equivalent of a tall man being nicknamed Shorty. Who can say?"

Vledder abandoned the subject. He looked pensive.

"But there's still something else I don't understand," he said.

"Out with it," invited DeKok.

"Why did Handsome Karl tell us he'd been in jail? That wasn't very smart. It would be so easy to check."

DeKok nodded.

"I think that Karl was a bit confused when I told him I had missed him for awhile. The excuse about jail time in The Hague was the first thing to pop into his mind. If he had told us he had been caretaking on an estate in Ireland, he knew we would discover his relation to Vreeden quickly."

"One more thing checked off," nodded Vledder with satisfaction. He moved in his chair and rubbed the back of his neck with a pained expression on his face as he wrestled with his questions. "Why would Archie Benson have to disappear? His fate is so senseless."

"You believe he's dead, then?" asked DeKok.

"Yes, I think so. Little Lowee thinks the same. Otherwise he would not have made so much noise. But what bothers me more than anything else is why."

"He knew too much."

Vledder shook his head.

"What fatal knowledge could he have? They never executed the plan. The cabin cruiser sits, unused, moored in the Amstel. DeKok, look at the facts. Not only was there no reason to murder Archie, he was handy to have around."

"How do you mean, handy?"

Vledder made a nonchalant gesture.

"Any number of things—he could run errands, move the boat. If there was a hostage, he could keep an eye on the victim, get food—"

"But those are tasks," said DeKok softly, "to do when there is an actual hostage. You said it yourself. There was no hostage, because there was no kidnapping."

Vledder was peeved.

"It could still happen," he exclaimed, nettled. "The plans were in place. The execution hadn't quite happened. And during the execution of the kidnapping, Archie would have been very useful, you'll admit that."

DeKok sighed.

"I think you're staring yourself dead with this."

Vledder looked up in surprise.

"What else is there? I'd gladly shift my focus."

"Think about a funeral."

"What funeral?"

His partner's lack of insight made DeKok close his eyes momentarily.

"What was Archie's big problem, just before he died?" he reminded, patiently. "Think about Archie's conversation with a couple of gangsters in Lowee's bar."

It took awhile, but then Vledder's face suddenly lit up.

"He was consumed with getting rid of a body."

DeKok looked at him for a few seconds.

"Are you with me, now?" he asked sarcastically. He stood up and ambled over to get his coat and hat. "Keep the thought for a little while longer."

His hand was reaching for his hat, when the phone on his desk rang.

Vledder, who had started to follow DeKok, picked up the phone and listened.

DeKok watched from a distance. He saw Vledder's face become grave. Slowly the old man walked back to his desk.

When Vledder had replaced the receiver, DeKok looked at him.

"What was it?"

"A notification," said Vledder dully. "We're needed."

"Yes," urged DeKok impatiently.

"Dr. Haanstra is dead."

"Murdered?"

"Yes," said Vledder, "strangled with a scarf."

17

Vledder ran headlong down the stairs, three steps at a time. DeKok tightened the belt of his raincoat and followed at a more sedate pace. Downstairs Vledder waited impatiently for his partner to catch up. As they crossed the lobby, the watch commander beckoned them with a crooked finger.

"Are you going after the dead doctor?"

DeKok looked annoyed.

"Yes, what is it?"

Jan Kuster waved at the notes spread on his desk.

"There's a patrol car in front of the doctor's house. As soon as you get there please send them back. Just look at this," he said sadly, "it is a manpower crisis. I have all these requests for assistance, but nobody left on the shift to send. Those bureaucrats in The Hague had better figure out how to clone cops." Unsmiling, he looked up.

"There's one detective left upstairs," volunteered Vledder. "Perhaps you can use him."

"Thanks. I'll check. Don't forget to send the patrol back."

The inspectors waved on their way out.

Once outside, Vledder headed for the car, but DeKok held him back.

"Leave the car, perhaps Kuster can use it. He has

enough trouble. We can walk it in less time then you can get that thing going."

Vledder reluctantly complied.

"You're not quite a marathon walker, you know," he remarked.

"Dead is dead," said DeKok. He glanced at Vledder. "Or do you think that by rushing you can bring him back to life?"

Vledder did not respond, but walked ahead of DeKok. The young man always had difficulty controlling his impatience with DeKok's shuffle. But he had to admit DeKok, thanks to his intimate knowledge of his city, often arrived at his destination before any car or bicycle could.

DeKok lifted his hat to a young heroin whore. In recent months she became a regular in the waiting room at Warmoes Street. She was an anemic looking little woman, who sat quietly. She looked around with dull eyes, waiting to be interrogated or processed. He recalled she was German, but could not remember her name. He turned his head and looked at her thoughtfully as she disappeared around the corner.

She was the symbol of an entire army. The population of addicts increased incrementally. Certainly the Amsterdam Municipal Police could not stem the tide. An enlightened drug policy of the government had succeeded in reducing the number of new addicts by about ninety percent. This percentage, however, was reflective of the Dutch population only. The removal of border restrictions by the EU, coupled with the legalization of drugs in the Netherlands, resulted in a flood of foreigners. They flocked to Dutch population centers such as Amsterdam. Soft drugs were readily available in coffee shops, openly sold from menus.

Hard drugs required more effort, but not much more. Sooner or later, mused DeKok, something must be done to stem the flow of hard drugs and victims of this trade. He smiled wanly. It would be for the new generation of legislators and cops to address. He had not many years remaining until retirement.

DeKok's progress was deceptive. Vledder waited for him at the corner of Warmoes Street. His face was red.

"We're on the way to a murder," he said in a harsh voice. "You *do* remember?"

DeKok nodded, resigned.

"Right—we have an appointment with a dead doctor."

When they reached Emperor's Canal, Vledder glanced at his watch. He had to admit they were there at least five minutes earlier than if they had taken the car. They climbed the bluestone steps. A bored, uniformed constable leaned against a doorpost. When he noticed DeKok, he hastily took a step forward and saluted.

"She's in the waiting room, sir."

DeKok looked puzzled.

"Who are you talking about?"

The cleaning woman, I mean the interior caretaker, who discovered the murder. She has a key. When she came around eight o'clock to clean, she noticed the door was unlocked and ajar. The front door is always locked outside of consulting hours. At first she thought it was a burglary. Before she telephoned the police it occurred to her the doctor might have just forgotten to close the door. She went in."

"That's when she found him."

"Yes."

"You have her name?"

DeKok was pleased to see the constable take a notebook out of his pocket and consult it.

"Anne-Marie Schild, unmarried, age fifty-seven. She's been working for the doctor ever since he opened his practice here on the canal."

"Particulars concerning the victim?"

"Haanstra ... that's all I have."

"Touch anything inside?"

The young constable shook his head.

"I did think about looking for identification on the corpse. But I thought it better to leave it to you. We didn't have to touch the body. It is clear from a distance he's history ... dead. It isn't just the scarf around his neck. His tongue is black and it's hanging out. Not pretty." He sighed. Then he looked at the inspector with a question in his eyes. "Do you want me to alert anybody for you, sir?"

"No, thank you. Good report. The watch commander is alerting the Herd. He wants you to come right back. He's stretched pretty thin. He needs you."

"Very good, sir," said the constable. He saluted again and walked down the steps to join his even younger colleague, who was guarding the radio in the patrol car.

Before he reached the bottom of the steps, DeKok called him.

"Hey!"

The constable turned around at the foot of the steps and looked up.

"Sir?" he asked.

"What's with the sirs and the saluting?" demanded DeKok. "You wouldn't be having fun at my expense?"

The constable looked perplexed.

"No, sir," he said. "You're Inspector DeKok."

He said it as though it explained everything.

DeKok blushed.

"Oh," he said. "Thank you."

"Yes, sir," said the constable, who saluted again and walked to the car.

Vledder grinned.

"Your fame is spreading," he leered.

"Never mind," grumbled DeKok and turned toward the door.

Suddenly he halted and took a second look at the brass plate next to the door.

"J. E. Haanstra," he read out loud, "consultation hours from ten until noon." He turned to Vledder, his face even. "Where do you think the doctor will hold his consultations tomorrow, heaven or hell?"

"Hell," said Vledder without hesitation. "It's more than likely his destination."

"Why?"

Vledder looked serious.

"Be honest, DeKok. If you were God, would you allow people in your heaven?"

The gray sleuth did not answer. He pushed open the door and stepped inside.

Vledder followed.

While the younger inspector interviewed a hysterical charwoman, DeKok let his sharp gaze drift around the consultation room. He took it all in with photographic precision, the brown leather examination couch, the antique scales, an oaken measuring stick, and the dead doctor in his chair behind the desk.

The young constable was right. It was a specter from a nightmare. The swollen face, protruding tongue, and bulging eyes offered a gruesome sight. The doctor's face was forever frozen in terror.

DeKok shook his head in despair. As with Marlies van Haesbergen, he felt a sense of guilt. Should he have been able to prevent this? His mind accepted his limitations. Dutch law had not left him any other choice. But his heart told him he had failed these two people.

Vledder entered the room.

"I've sent the poor woman home," he said. "She's confused and upset. She's known the doctor since he was a baby. She was a housekeeper in his parents' home."

"Did she add anything to her account?"

"No, she told me the same thing she told the constable. She did suggest the doctor must have been killed by someone who had an appointment outside of surgery hours."

"Why did she say that?"

"He's still wearing his white coat. The charwoman said he hated the white coat, called it his uniform. He always took it off as soon as possible. He preferred casual clothes."

DeKok pointed at the file box on the desk.

"Take that with you, when we leave. Meanwhile, look around and see if you can find the patient card for Vreeden."

"It isn't there?"

"No," said DeKok grimly. "It wasn't in there this afternoon." He pointed at the wastepaper basket next to the desk. "Check that out, as well. If I'm right, you'll find a torn up card with an inkblot over my name."

Vledder nodded to himself and made some entries in his notebook. Then he took a good look at the corpse.

"Not a flattering pose—in fact, that's what you call macabre."

"He struggled."

"How can you tell?"

"He's no longer seated in the chair. He's hanging in it. I think there must have been a short struggle. When the strangler approached him from the back, the doctor must have tried to get up."

"And then sank back down."

"Precisely."

Vledder made some more notes and then looked at his partner.

"Do you have any idea *why* he was killed?"

DeKok nodded slowly.

"Yes, I know."

"You know?" Vledder inquired with surprise.

"Yes."

Vledder grinned uncertainly.

"Would you mind telling me—" he stopped short. Dr. Koning suddenly appeared in the door opening. The morgue attendants stood behind him looking like bodyguards, the stretcher upright between them.

DeKok walked over to the old doctor.

"You're first again."

Dr. Koning smiled wryly.

"My parents were grocers. They taught me to take care of my best clients." He walked around DeKok and approached the chair with the victim. With his hands in his pockets he looked for a long time.

"Has he been photographed?"

"No."

Dr. Koning leaned over the victim and closed the eyes.

He gave DeKok a slight smile.

"Why should we scare the poor photographer with that frightful stare? Even with closed eyes he's pretty repulsive."

Dr. Koning went through his usual ritual with his pince-nez. After he had cleaned it to his satisfaction, he looked at DeKok.

"By the way ... he's dead."

DeKok shrugged.

"I suspected it."

The coroner hesitated for a moment. There was a pensive look in his eyes.

"You had, I believe, a previous strangulation—the elderly woman from a few days ago. Wasn't she also strangled with a scarf?"

"Indeed."

Dr. Koning nodded to himself.

"I thought as much." He paused. "Although I don't like to jump to conclusions, you'd be well advised to look for the same person. The *modus operandi* are identical. The pathologist will confirm it, but it might give you a head start, so to speak."

"Thank you, doctor," said DeKok, always grateful for whatever morsel of knowledge the old coroner chose to share. The man must have seen more corpses than just about anybody else in Amsterdam, with the possible exception of some funeral parlor operators. The thought prompted him to ask a question.

"Aside from personal reasons, why would someone want to kill a doctor?"

Koning's response was tongue-in-cheek.

"Perhaps he made the wrong diagnosis," he smiled. "An occupational hazard."

"Has it ever happened to you?"

"You mean, that I declared somebody dead, while he was still alive?"

"It could happen."

Dr. Koning shook his head. He threw another pensive look in the direction of the corpse. Then he lifted his old Garibaldi hat in respect and left the room. DeKok suddenly realized that the old man had not lifted his hat when he first saw the corpse. He usually did that. Was it just an oversight at the end of a long, tiring day? While DeKok debated silently, Bram Weelen stormed into the room.

The photographer placed his aluminum suitcase on the floor. He spoke to DeKok over his shoulder.

"What do you want?"

"What do you mean ... *what do I want?*"

"What kind of pictures, of course," said Bram, lifting the Hasselblad from its foam rubber nest.

DeKok did not answer, but waited until Weelen stood up and faced him.

"What's the matter with you?" asked DeKok. His tone was prickly. "Are you in a hurry again? Last time I hardly saw you. You flew in and out like a shadow."

Bram looked apologetic.

"I want to run over to the hospital. My eldest daughter delivered a baby yesterday. It wasn't an easy delivery. There were some complications." His face lit up and he grinned from ear to ear. "But it's a wonder of a boy! He weighed in at seven pounds, three ounces. He's always hungry and has lungs of leather." He patted DeKok on the shoulder. "And I tell you something else, they named him after me."

DeKok smiled.

"Congratulations. Now you're a role model."

Weelen spread both arms, his precious Hasselblad hanging precariously from the tips of his fingers.

"Don't you think it's wonderful?"

DeKok nodded.

"How's your daughter?"

"Good, we think she can come home tomorrow."

DeKok looked at the corpse.

"I just want a few pictures. His face ... the scarf ... the knot ... the way he's hanging in the chair. After that, you may leave, as far as I'm concerned."

Weelen gave him a grateful look and went to work.

Before Bram had his first exposure, Kruger came in. He looked around. His face was somber.

"My luck with prints has gone from bad to worse lately," he said unhappily. "It's an epidemic—every criminal is wearing gloves. It's because all those idiotic detective novels—"

He was interrupted by a triumphant yell from Vledder. With a wide card in his hand, he crawled away from the desk. He stood up and walked over to DeKok.

"Found it! It wasn't in the trash; it was under the desk, near the wall. It must have fallen during the struggle and slid across the wooden floor under the desk."

DeKok took the card and studied it. It was the same kind of card the doctor had begun for him. In the block under "Name", the letters K. Ko. appeared.

Vledder looked over DeKok's shoulder.

"Karl Koperman."

18

It was well after midnight when they returned to the station house. After the morgue attendants had taken the corpse away, Ben Kruger had taken his time. Obsessed by the desire to find usable prints, he had just about covered the entire consultation room in gray aluminum powder. As he started toward the waiting room, DeKok had resolutely sent him away, suitcase and all. At just about that time the Herd and the rest of the CSI team arrived. Vledder and DeKok had left almost on Kruger's heels.

Exhausted, DeKok sank down in the chair behind his desk. His face was drawn, the features skewed with pain. He lifted his legs to rest them on the desktop.

"Kruger is taking it over the top, these days," he grumbled. "He was ready to dust everything including the ceiling fan. Fingerprints are his whole world."

Vledder did not react. He waved a plastic bag around. In it was the scarf from the second strangling.

"When are we going to arrest him?"

Listlessly, DeKok looked up.

"Who?"

The young inspector beheld his older colleague in utter amazement.

"Handsome Karl," he exclaimed, irritation in his voice. "Karl Koperman. It's clear as day he presented himself as a patient, to gain access to the doctor. Then he strangled him."

DeKok did not move.

"You mean," he murmured, "because of that card with K. Ko?"

"Yes, what else?"

DeKok closed his eyes, as if asking for patience.

"What else?" asked DeKok.

"I mean," said Vledder impatiently, "we know the details of his attempted strangling of Fat Nellie. We know someone succeeded in strangling Marlies van Haesbergen with a scarf. You have as much evidence as you need for probable cause."

"You think so?"

"Of course, and anybody would agree with me. What else do you want?"

"Nothing else … just to catch the real killer."

Vledder's face turned red.

"The real killer," he repeated with a sneer. He pointed at the plastic bag. "Handsome Karl *is* the real killer."

DeKok pulled out his lower lip and let it plop back. He did it again. When he tried to do it once more, he stopped, because Vledder interrupted him.

"Stop it," cried Vledder. "Enough is enough. What about the real killer?"

DeKok looked at his partner through half-closed eyes.

"Why," he said reasonably, "should K. Ko have to mean Karl Koperman?" His eyes closed almost completely. "It could just as easily mean Kees Koster, or Krelis Kolenshouwer, need I go on? A smart lawyer, certainly a man like Meturovski, sweeps evidence like that off the table. He'll enjoy the joke, and the court will not be able to stop him."

He paused a moment. A twinkle appeared in his eyes as he opened them all the way. "A self-respecting defense council could use the K. Ko to Karl's benefit."

Vledder was stunned.

"What are you saying?"

DeKok took his legs off the desk and stood up. He perfectly imitated the stance and gestures of a barrister pleading a case in court.

"What man, your honors," he declaimed with just the right degree of drama, "what man plans a murder and hands his intended victim an opportunity to write, or begin to write, what will become an engraved invitation to the police? I ask you, your honors, would we expect even the stupidest criminal to participate in his own demise?"

Vledder pointed at the floor.

"The card was on the floor—the murderer did not mean it to be found."

DeKok nodded resignedly.

"Think about it."

The young inspector shook his head.

"I'm done," he growled obstreperously. "We'll never unravel it."

DeKok did not react. He looked pensively at his colleague for several seconds. Then he turned around and went to get his coat.

Vledder shook himself and followed.

"Now where are you going?"

DeKok yawned widely.

"Home. I need sleep. Pick me up at nine o'clock with a car."

"Where are we going tomorrow?"

"Amersfoort."

Vledder stood still and wrinkled his forehead as he thought. He apparently had forgotten his oath not to think anymore.

"What do you want to do there?"

DeKok's face was hard and pitiless.

"Get to the bottom of things."

Although the rush hour was supposed to be over, the four-lane Beltway around Amsterdam was still congested. Vledder kept the VW at a sedate pace in the curb lane. He watched placidly as other traffic switched lanes and rushed past. Accustomed to Vledder's heavy foot, DeKok couldn't help remarking on the sedate pace.

"Why are you going so slow?" he asked.

"I'm not going slow," answered Vledder. "I'm doing the speed limit. I could step on it and get into the middle of the melee, but I would have to step on my brakes as often as I use the gas pedal, just to pass." He pointed at a sleek Jaguar that passed them in the next lane. "See, this is the third time that Jag has passed me. Within half a kilometer I'll pass him again without accelerating or using my brakes."

"Isn't this a big change in your technique?"

"Not really. This isn't the city and I'm not using my siren or lights. I'm keeping an eye on that truck," he pointed out the windshield. "That's a professional driver, who probably runs this route frequently. Notice how he stays in the curb lane? As long as I've been behind him, he hasn't used his brakes and hasn't changed speed. People naturally assume a truck is slow and do anything to get past him. As a result he, and his truck-driving buddies, take the curb lane for themselves. They are zipping right along." He paused.

"And so are we," he added with a satisfied smirk.

They reached their turn-off for Amersfoort and Utrecht. The traffic thinned out. After Vledder's explanation, DeKok almost regretted that the truck they had been following continued on past the exit.

Vledder glanced to one side. DeKok was still sitting upright. He had not yet sunk down in the seat in his usual slumped attitude.

"By the way," said Vledder, "I had to go by the station to get the car and fuel."

"Eh?"

"In the lobby, after I had signed out on the log, I almost ran smack into our commissaris. He immediately wanted to know your whereabouts. The second strangulation has him and the judge advocate seriously worried."

"Is that what he said?"

Vledder nodded. He checked his mirrors and glanced at the dashboard.

"Yes," he said. "Also," he went on, "Mr. Meturovski is stirring up trouble again. Although he has withdrawn his complaint against us, he has expressed his genuine reluctance to approve of our behavior. Apparently you made unfounded statements to poor Mr. Middelkoop. He was extremely upset by your veiled accusations."

"Ah, so," said DeKok. "No surprise there."

Vledder looked serious.

"There's more. Urged on by Messrs. Grauw and Middelkoop, Meturovski beseeched the commissaris and Mr. Schaap to assign the Vreeden case to other inspectors in the precinct. According to Mr. Meturovski, our integrity is suspect, at the very least. The primary omission appears to have objectivity—we displayed a certain prejudice."

DeKok narrowed his eyes.

"That's interesting. Meturovski admits there is indeed a Vreeden case."

"Apparently."

DeKok laughed out loud.

"That is priceless! Until now the attitude in the firm was, 'Mr., Vreeden is on vacation in the Bahamas.' This is the first time they have wavered. I have the warm feeling they are getting a teeny wee bit worried."

Vledder snorted.

"Of course ... with all that rooting around you're doing."

DeKok's face fell.

"I'm afraid that my rooting around has cost two lives, so far."

Vledder shook his head.

"That's absolute nonsense," he cried out. "None of it is on your head. You didn't get a scarf and strangle two people. Someone else chose to forever silence them."

DeKok stared out of the window. He imagined the frightening visage of the dead Dr. Haanstra in his mind's eye. With an effort he pushed the image away.

"When we get back to Amsterdam," he said slowly, "I want you to go have a look at the city register."

"In person?"

"Yes, that seems safer and more discrete than calling. I'd like you to check out Karl Koperman's family, grandparents, uncles, aunts, cousins, nephews, nieces, ... the works."

"What do you plan to do with the data?"

DeKok sighed.

"I want to know who got him the caretaker job at Thundering Heights in Ireland. According to Lowee,

Handsome Karl has connections in high places."

"And that's what you want me to find?"

"In a round about way," said DeKok.

They remained silent for a long time. Past Bussum, visibility became worse. Patches of thick fog dressed the world in a gray blanket. Vledder cursed to himself, engaged the fog lights, and slowed down.

"Is she home?" he asked gruffly.

"Who?"

"Xaveria, of course. Isn't that why we're going to Amersfoort?"

DeKok nodded.

"I called her this morning. I asked her to stay at home because we had an important message for her."

"We do?"

"Yes."

Vledder did not persist. Suddenly he put his hand in the inside pocket of his coat.

"I almost forgot," he said sheepishly. "There was an envelope for you at the watch commander's desk. It was delivered during the night."

DeKok looked at the much-folded envelope and studied the address: "To Inspector DeKok, Warmoes Street Police Station," written in neat, copperplate script. He tore open the envelope and produced a sheet of notepaper.

Dear DeKok,

It took a while, but now I know for sure. Handsome Karl has not left the city. He's hiding out in a renovated townhouse in Zaan Street, next to the old swimming pool building. In front is a fire-engine-red BMW he owns. He almost never shows himself in the street. It seems he is a bit nervous. If you want to catch him,

you should hurry, or he may be gone.
Yours, Louis

DeKok smiled tenderly and put the note and the envelope into one of his pockets.

"Good news?" asked Vledder.

"Yes, it's from Lowee."

"What, with that handwriting?"

"Oh, yes. And the note is in the same perfect copperplate script and in perfect Dutch, not a misspelling either."

"So, he doesn't write the way he speaks?"

"No, and if he wanted he could give elocution lessons
to radio announcers. As we discussed, it would never be a
good idea to underestimate the man."

She wore the same, almost transparent, dressing gown
she had worn during their first visit to Amersfoort. Again
DeKok realized how attractive she was, how exciting.
Everytime he encountered her he understood more of the
spellbinding enchantment Vreeden must have experienced.

Xaveria Breerode gave him a haughty look.

"It seems I'm to enjoy your frequent interest," she
mocked.

DeKok smiled a winning smile.

"Believe me, if I didn't have a real reason for my visit,
I'd invent a motive to visit you."

"Is that a compliment?" she asked, flattered.

DeKok nodded with conviction.

"A compliment to your beauty. I admire your candor
rather less."

Suddenly there was an alert look in her eyes.

"I am unaware of having withheld anything. If so it was completely inadvertent."

DeKok pointed an accusing finger at her.

"Why did you not tell us, during our last visit, that you're Paul Vreeden's sole beneficiary and his executrix? That is no small omission."

She feigned innocence.

"You did not ask."

DeKok pursed his lips before speaking.

"Surely you understood how important it was for us to know. It was key to our investigation."

She shook her head.

"No, it simply did not seem relevant. My only concern, really, was, and is, Paul's disappearance. I did *not* realize that. Our financial arrangements have no bearing."

"Oh, no?" It was DeKok's turn to sound mocking.

Her face became hard.

"Listen carefully, Inspector," she said bitingly, "all I want or need is Mr. Vreeden to be safe and whole. But you know that—it is your job."

The gray sleuth ignored the remark.

"What sort of relationship do you have with Gerard Grauw?"

"None whatsoever."

DeKok grinned, but only with his mouth. His gaze was one of unflattering assessment.

"Yesterday morning we saw him leave your house."

"He was here," she admitted calmly. "Shortly before you came, he appeared in front of my door."

"You invited him in?"

"No, I permitted him to enter. There is a difference."

"What did he want?"

Xaveria Breerode lowered her head slightly, her poise was slipping.

"Grauw told me he had received a copy of Paul's will. He wanted to discuss the contents with me."

"And?"

"I made it clear I did not intend to discuss the contents with him, as the will was Mr. Vreeden's last testament, not mine. If Grauw wanted changes made to the will, for whatever reason, I said he should direct his desires to Paul."

DeKok was amused. He thoroughly enjoyed her recollection of thwarting Grauw, whom he considered a cold fish.

"What was his response?"

"He gave me the feeling he was severely upset. He had difficulty keeping his composure—shut his briefcase with a smack, stood up, and left without saying goodbye."

DeKok rubbed his chin thoughtfully. There was something here, if he could only put his finger on it. He searched Xaveria's face for inspiration.

"During our last visit," he began after a long pause, "you ... gave us a character sketch of Mr. Vreeden. You told us about his giving away 1,000 Euro notes in conjunction with overseas negotiations."

"You remembered that?" laughed Xaveria.

"Yes," nodded DeKok. "You also spoke of a unique shirt with pockets in which he transported currency. You have an example of that?"

Xaveria stood up and walked over to a tall chest.

"The night before he left for the Near East," she said, "Paul spent the night with me. He joked about it giving him resistance against the wiles of the *Houris*. Shortly before he left for the airport, he would transform himself into a slightly rounder gentleman."

"He became so because of all the currency on his body?"

She grinned as she opened a drawer.

"It looked quite natural, but I found it a bit comical. I always had to laugh when I saw him like that." She took a piece of clothing out of the drawer and held it up. It was a rather long T-shirt with pockets stitched all around in three rows, one under the other. DeKok reached out for it.

"Do you mind if I show this to my commissaris?" he asked.

She hesitated for a moment.

"As long as I get it back."

"Absolutely."

She handed the odd garment to the inspector, and closed the drawer. Then she reseated herself on a hassock.

"When Paul comes back, he'll need it," she said.

DeKok nodded soothingly. He folded the garment neatly and stuck into his raincoat, over the belt. Laboriously he stood up. But he did not leave.

"Would you share with me," he asked, "how you met Mr. Vreeden for the first time?"

"We were introduced by friends."

"What friends?"

"I ... I don't recall. It was a long time ago."

DeKok made an inviting gesture in her direction, as if to solicit a further answer. She did not respond.

"Presumably you still remember the happy day?" he asked.

She swallowed. Her tongue darted out and licked dry lips.

"Not really, I don't remember details."

DeKok held her eyes with his own.

"Did you know Mr. Grauw before he came to work with Mr. Vreeden as a co-director in the firm?"

Xaveria did not answer. She closed her eyes and sighed.

DeKok leaned closer to her.

"I know you heard me and understood me. But let me repeat myself. Did you know Mr. Grauw before he came to work with Mr. Vreeden as a co-director in the firm?"

"Yes."

"Was Grauw the man who introduced you to Vreeden?"

She stood up. There was a hunted look in her eyes.

"That has nothing to do with anything," she declared, emotionally. "Regardless of who introduced us, I love Paul ... believe me ... I love him." She fell silent. She appeared to be drained of all emotion. Dully she looked up at DeKok. "I know what you think," she whispered.

There was no expression on DeKok's face.

"We cannot always control our thoughts," he said. Slowly he walked away. At the door he turned around.

"Do you have mourning clothes?"

"No."

"Buy some."

19

They left Amersfoort from the familiar parking lot on Precious Lady Square. The visibility on the highway had improved. The sun had climbed high in the sky and had burned off the last of the fog.

DeKok slid down in the seat and almost dozed off. Sleepily he reviewed the conversation with Xaveria. It had progressed more or less along the lines he had expected. No real surprises there. The first time he observed Grauw leaving her street he knew there must be some bond between him and Xaveria.

He was still puzzled by the sequence of events. Had the love affair between Xaveria and Paul led to a directorship for Grauw? Or had the directorship of Grauw led to the intimate relationship between Paul and the enticing Xaveria Breerode? Which was cause and which was effect? During his questioning, Xaveria admitted it was Grauw who had introduced her to Vreeden. In that case the initiative would have been Grauw's. DeKok wondered what prompted the writing and publishing of Paul Vreeden's recent last will and testament. He thought about Vreeden's instructions to his solicitor.

Vledder nudged him with an elbow.

"Are you asleep?"

DeKok pushed himself more upright.

"No, I was thinking with my eyes closed."

"Well, at least you weren't snoring." He pointed at the bulge under DeKok's raincoat. "What do you want with that shirt?"

"As I said, I have it to show to the commissaris."

Vledder snorted.

"And you really think he'll be interested?"

DeKok jutted his chin forward.

"It will arouse his interest." It sounded hard and inflexible.

"Why?"

The gray sleuth turned in the seat, almost facing Vledder.

"You've been a part of the entire investigation," he said tiredly. "From the start, you've been involved with all the facets of the case. Now, what do you think I want with this shirt?"

Vledder shoulders rose momentarily.

"I have no clue. Perhaps you want to use it in a training lecture for Her Majesty's customs."

Disappointed, DeKok shook his head. With a sad expression on his face he sank back in the seat and closed his eyes. This time he did nod off. They were back in Amsterdam before he woke up.

"When we get to Town Hall, leave the car with me," he ordered. "Do you have the correct information about Karl Koperman and his mother for the registry?"

"Yes ... but you, eh, you're going to drive?"

"Of course," said DeKok in a matter-of-fact tone of voice. He knew he'd distinguished himself as the worst driver in the Netherlands, maybe all of Europe. He also knew that Vledder thought the same. He behaved as though he had a flawless driving record. "I'll see you at the station," he added.

"You're just going to drive to the station?"

"Well, no, I think I'll pay a little visit to the notary, Sugtelen."

"You're going to *park* along Gentlemen's Canal?"

"Yes, why not?" he said, blandly. "That's where his office is located."

"Alright, try not to park it *in* the canal."

They reached Town Hall and Vledder prepared to get out of the car.

"Why are you going to see the notary?"

"I want to have a look at the report the detective in Amersfoort prepared."

"And if he refuses to show it to you?"

"Why should he refuse?"

"Notaries can be very secretive."

DeKok waved that away.

"It's not all that important. Besides, I have another, more enjoyable job."

"What kind of job?"

A malicious grin played across DeKok's face.

"I'm simply going to issue a polite invitation to our commissaris. I'm going to ask him and his superior, Judge Advocate Schaap, to a discussion at the Warmoes Street Station. They're certain to accept because of my newfound subservient attitude."

"You're leading this discussion?"

"Yes, I need his help."

Vledder almost fell out of the half-open door of the car.

"You," he exclaimed in bewilderment, *"you* are going to ask the judge advocate for help?"

"It's just encouraging him to do his job; after all he'll gladly take credit."

Vledder shook his head and left the car. He stood on the sidewalk and watched DeKok leave. The VW lurched forward, clutch slipping, gears grinding, engine whining. After a second lurch it roared off. He shook his head again as he turned around to enter Town Hall.

DeKok darted a quick tongue over his dry lips. Tension made the tips of his fingers tingle. He loosened his tie and looked at the large clock on the wall. It was almost nine o'clock. Almost an hour and a half separated him from decisive action.

He reflected. If anything went wrong this time he would loose his last chance to shed some light on the mysterious disappearance of Paul Vreeden. Simultaneously he would fail in making the connection between what had befallen Vreeden and the murders of Marlies van Haesbergen and Dr. Haanstra. He shivered, painfully aware of the risks he ran.

DeKok looked around the detective room. All the regular desks were empty, but a small group was seated around his desk. To his left was Vledder, looking wan. Sitting on the edge of Vledder's desk were Fred Prins and Els Rijpke. The two were young, capable, and committed. Prins was tall and brunette, a muscular Indonesian. Rijpke was tall, as well, but lithe and blonde. DeKok had requested the assistance of the two sergeant inspectors, who had enthusiastically offered to help.

DeKok had pled his case with Buitendam and Schaap with humility and candor. He had explained in careful detail the results of his investigations and his plans for obtaining incontrovertible evidence.

His quiet gravity caught their attention and kept it. At least for now, they had abandoned the interruptions and non-sequiturs. After an exhausting debate, they had approved his plans. Mr. Schaap had even gone so far as to state that, in the event of a complete failure, he would assume total responsibility for DeKok's actions.

Commissaris Buitendam had committed a number of very fast cars to the operation. With a sigh of relief, DeKok had left the company of his commanding officer.

He'd have liked to surprise Vledder. After some consideration, he decided to give his partner all the details of his plan. He also wanted Vledder to share his ultimate goal. After the briefing, young Vledder stared at his old friend with utter amazement. He called him a "Crony of the Devil." Giving credit where it was due he admitted he'd never have come up with an idea this brilliant.

DeKok looked up and turned to Appie Keizer, an older colleague, who was leaning against a wall, sipping a cup of coffee.

"Why don't you go down to dispatch," he said. "I don't expect anything to happen before quarter after ten, but you never know. I also have a car on standby with Klaver and Kuip. As soon as they report in, let me know at once."

Inspector Keizer drained his cup of coffee, placed the empty mug on a nearby desk, and walked out of the room.

DeKok looked at the others.

"Let's take our posts." His voice trembled just a bit. "Waiting up here is making me nervous."

Prins and Rijpke stood up and followed Keizer out of the room.

Vledder approached DeKok.

"What if they know it's a set-up?"

The older man shrugged.

"I'm counting on their greed."

DeKok caressed the interior of the car with his eyes. The car had been confiscated as part of a drug bust. His hands stroked the luxurious upholstery. He wasn't used to this kind of comfort in police cars. He leaned back and nestled himself comfortably into the passenger seat. It was a cozy feeling. He peered out of the windshield and saw the silhouette of Haarlem Gate.

Vledder glanced aside.

"Is this a good place?"

DeKok shrugged.

"We could have positioned ourselves just about anywhere. I've no idea where they'll lead. Haarlem Square seemed best. What's the time?"

Vledder pointedly studied the digital clock on the dashboard.

"About ten past ten," he said.

DeKok sighed impatiently.

"Things should develop shortly. The APB must have been sent out at least ten minutes ago."

"What if our target audience didn't watch?"

"I've been assured that the ten o'clock news is the most watched program in Holland. The APB must have been the first item on the menu. And these people are sure to watch the news."

The radio hummed slightly and then the voice of Keizer came on the net.

"Base to Alpha: Car Beta reports a black Cadillac sedan

approaching the Coen Tunnel. It is proceeding at a high speed."

Vledder looked at his partner.

"That's Klaver and Kuip," said DeKok. "Ask if they can keep up." Vledder lifted the microphone and made the call. The answer took several seconds.

"Base to Alpha: Out of contact with Beta. They're probably inside the tunnel."

They waited. Then Keizer's voice came back on the air.

"Base to all Units: Cadillac has left harbor area and is passing Telegraph Building in direction of Canal F for Fox."

DeKok looked at Vledder. The map of Amsterdam was clearly imprinted in his mind.

"He's going in the direction of Velsen," he murmured. Then, without waiting for Vledder, DeKok grabbed the microphone.

"Any news about Prins and Rijpke?" he asked, ignoring all radio procedures. Keizer came back after a few seconds.

"Base to Alpha: A red BMW just left Zaan Street in the direction of Haarlem Road. Delta in pursuit."

DeKok nudged Vledder in the ribs.

"Start her up," he growled, "Head straight for Haarlem Road."

The young inspector reacted at once. He laid rubber as he pulled the powerful Peugeot away from the curb. He narrowly missed a taxicab and entered the approaches to Nassau Bridge on two wheels. They had barely reached Nassau Square when a fire-engine-red BMW came from the right and took the corner to Haarlem Road on screeching tires. A blue Citroen followed at some distance. DeKok pointed at it.

"Is that Prins and Rijpke?"

"Yes," said Vledder. He reached for the microphone.

"Alpha to Base: Have Delta and pursued vehicle in sight on Nassau Square—in pursuit."

"Keep your distance," cautioned DeKok, "so they don't spot us. If Prins and Rijpke have to leave off, we can take up the pursuit ourselves."

Vledder did not bother to answer. He considered it a superfluous suggestion. DeKok must be tense, he thought.

They raced along narrow Haarlem Road at speeds exceeding 100 kilometers per hour. As they crossed Sloter Dike, the red BMW and the blue Citroen slipped through a yellow light. Vledder stopped on the red, cursing.

"You'd better get to confession," suggested DeKok. "Such language."

Vledder did not answer. As soon as the light switched to green, he floored the accelerator. The car tore away from the intersection. Within seconds they were at maximum speed. Before they reached the little town of Halfway, so called because it is exactly half way between Amsterdam and Haarlem, they had the blue Citroen in sight.

For long minutes they drove in silence. Then the radio gave its warning hum.

"Base to Alpha: Beta reports losing suspect vehicle. Base reports reception is getting weaker because of distance. Beta indicates pursued vehicle left highway in direction Bloemendaal. Delta reports they have you in sight."

DeKok slammed his fist on the dashboard.

"So," he exclaimed, "it's the Kemner Dunes, after all."

"I thought it was what you expected."

DeKok shook his head, but did not offer an explanation.

The blue Citroen's speed had leveled off. Vledder kept it in sight. They raced through the streets of Haarlem. When they took the turn to Bloemendaal, the Citroen sped up. DeKok only got only glimpses of the two vehicles.

"I hope our boys are careful," muttered DeKok, gripping the overhead strap tightly in his fist. "If those guys notice they're being followed, we can scrap the whole thing."

The Citroen was climbing a slight slope in the road. Just before the crest of the hill, the brake lights flashed on.

Vledder stopped as well. They had a clear view of the Kemner Dunes. They watched the red BMW, as it progressed slowly along the sandy edge of the foothills at the base of the dunes. The BMW flashed its headlights several times. The signal was answered by the flashing taillights of a black Cadillac. The BMW stopped close behind the larger car. A man left the BMW and walked over to the Cadillac. He opened the passenger door and climbed into the car. After a few seconds the Cadillac moved on down Sea Path.

DeKok motioned to Vledder. He drove to the blue Citroen and parked beside it. DeKok opened his window and looked at Fred Prins behind the wheel of the other car.

"Radios don't work, eh?"

"No, it's these damned city radios. We should have installed state police radios," said Prins.

"Don't worry. We're going to follow them. It's safer anyway. I don't think they have spotted us, but follow at a distance. Anything can happen."

Prins nodded.

"Any news of Klaver and Kuip?"

"No, last we heard they were losing contact with the Caddie. Their radios don't work, this far from the city, either."

"Very well, here we go."

Vledder switched off the lights and pressed the accelerator. The Peugeot followed the Cadillac. The white strip of sand made it fairly easy to navigate. The Cadillac moved slowly, as the driver searched the landscape. He pulled over within a mile or so. Vledder stopped at a discreet distance.

Both front doors of the Cadillac opened almost simultaneously. Two men alighted, slammed the doors behind them, and walked to the back of the car. They opened the trunk lid. As they walked toward the dunes each carried a shovel on his shoulders.

DeKok and Vledder got out of their car, leaving the doors open so as not to make a sound. Vledder had disabled the interior lights. Carefully bent over, they crept in the direction of the two men. Small bushes provided just enough cover. When they could see clearly, the two detectives fell flat on their stomachs in the sand. They observed.

The two men stopped as soon as they were out of sight of the road.

DeKok stared, but the darkness and the distance did not allow him to make a positive identification of either man.

Meanwhile the men discussed something. Then they started to dig. It was a macabre sight in the light of a pale moon.

Vledder started to get impatient. DeKok noticed and placed a calming hand on the young man's shoulder. "The more they dig," he whispered, "the less we have to do."

Vledder relaxed.

For a long time the men worked steadily. It grew harder

as they dug deeper. Their laborious breathing was clearly audible. No wonder, thought Vledder, the sand gets wetter and denser as you go deeper.

Suddenly something unforeseen happened. One of the men crawled out of the hole and pulled a pistol. Holding the weapon with both hands, he fired once, twice, three times at the man in the hole. The victim collapsed soundlessly.

Suddenly there was a lot of noise. Vledder jumped up. Shadows appeared from all directions.

Alarmed, the man next to the hole in the ground looked around. The pistol fell from his grasp. Frightened, he raised both hands in the air.

"Don't shoot …. don't shoot," he yelled.

DeKok scrambled upright. He had recognized the voice of Johan, Paul Vreeden's butler.

20

Vledder stood in front of the door and rang the bell. DeKok came out of his easy chair. He shuffled across the foyer in his slippers. After he had opened the door, he looked surprised.

"You're by yourself?"

Vledder nodded.

"The others couldn't come. They were snared by Narcotics for a raid."

DeKok shook his head in commiseration and led the young inspector to the cozily furnished living room.

Mrs. DeKok came out of the kitchen and greeted Vledder heartily.

The young inspector made an apologetic gesture.

"I regret I was unable to bring you flowers. By the time I woke up, all the shops were closed."

DeKok had a questioning look.

"What time did you finish?"

"It was already late in the afternoon before I got any sleep. The digging took a long time. It looked like archaeologists were unearthing some priceless artifact. At one point they even used brushes at the dig, if that's what you can call it."

"And, what did they eventually find?"

"They rested together, side by side, Paul Vreeden and

Archie Benson, in an eerie peace. Archie was shot execution style."

"What about Vreeden?"

Vledder spread his hands.

"He died of natural causes. Of course, there will be an official autopsy, but the Haarlem coroner was almost positive Vreeden died of a heart attack." He looked at DeKok. "What is Handsome Karl's status?"

The old man hung his head.

"He died this morning in the hospital."

"Did you talk to him?"

DeKok nodded slowly.

"He saw me inside the ambulance. Shortly before he died, he asked for me. Without any prompting, he told me that he had shot Archie and buried him next to Vreeden. He also confessed to the murder of Marlies van Haesbergen. When I mentioned Dr. Haanstra, he denied having had a hand in that. He claimed his brother was the killer."

Vledder swallowed in surprise.

"He had a brother, who was a murderer?" he asked.

DeKok did not answer, but pointed at one of the easy chairs across from his own.

"Let's sit down," he said wearily. "I haven't had more than a couple of hours sleep, myself."

He fell into the chair. He lifted a snifter of cognac from the little table next to his chair. He raised the glass.

"Cognac and a cold shower can work wonders."

Vledder was still bemused.

"Brother?" he wondered out loud.

"Yes," said DeKok. "First, before I explain, let me pour you a drink." He walked over to the sideboard and returned with another snifter and a bottle of cognac. Still standing he poured a generous measure in the glass and handed it to Vledder. Then he sat down again and refilled his own glass. He kept the bottle nearby.

Both men took small, appreciative sips.

"Yes," said DeKok after Vledder had lowered his glass. "Did you notice a resemblance? Johan the butler and Handsome Karl were brothers. I did not know until this afternoon, when I had a chance to look at the family records you brought me. I was floored to find out Mathilde had a second husband, a Cornelis Mindere, and a son out of that union, Johan Mindere."

Vledder still looked bewildered.

"I don't get it."

"Here's how I figured it out," said DeKok. When Commissaris Buitendam told me about the complaints against us for illegal entry by Meturovski, he spoke of a witness, Johan Mindere, the butler who had found us in Vreeden's place."

"Johan the butler … don't tell me the butler did it."

DeKok raked his fingers through his gray hair.

"From the moment I knew Karl had *not* been in jail, but had spent some time in Ireland, I was intrigued to know how he had managed to get the job as caretaker. That was important, you understand? Whoever referred him connected Paul Vreeden, Handsome Karl, and Black Archie, setting the wheels in motion for a kidnapping. That individual, man or woman, was central in the ensuing events."

Mrs. DeKok entered the room with a large plate of delicacies.

"You know what I don't understand," she said sweetly, "is why those men went to dig up the two corpses. Otherwise there would have been no way for them to be discovered."

DeKok looked scandalized.

"Corpses belong in a cemetery, not in the sand dunes."

Mrs. DeKok ignored her husband, but looked at Vledder.

"My husband did not answer my question—why unbury the bodies?"

"The corpses didn't interest them at all," laughed Vledder. "They were on a kind of treasure hunt."

"Buried treasure?"

Vledder pointed at DeKok.

"It was your husband's idea, a trick. He got the judge advocate, Mr. Schaap, to agree to broadcast an APB. They showed Vreeden's passport, with photo, and a very unique shirt with pockets. It was suggested Mr. Vreeden customarily carried approximately a million dollars in diverse currencies."

Mrs. DeKok looked down on her husband.

"So the two men were actually unburying the million?"

"Yes."

"And it wasn't true?"

Her husband smiled.

"It had a basis in truth. Paul Vreeden actually used undershirts with pockets sewn into them to carry large amounts of cash. He took cash with him when he traveled for his firm. There's no doubt it was bribe money."

"You mislead them in a kind of confidence game?"

DeKok bowed his head.

"I did."

Mrs. DeKok looked disapproving.

"Jurriaan DeKok, you're a—"

"He's a Crony of the Devil," Vledder interjected.

DeKok looked confused.

"Didn't you see the APB?"

Mrs. DeKok shook her head, as she placed the platter of food on the sideboard.

"No, I usually find the news depressing—crime, war, and disasters. I prefer to scan the headlines in the paper. Then I decide what I want to know."

She arranged some plates and cutlery on the sideboard, next to the food.

"You two should eat something with all that liquor," she advised. "Come Dick, see if there's anything you like."

Vledder stood up and made a selection. Mrs. DeKok heaped a plate for her husband. Soon she had gathered up some croquettes, some satays, an assortment of cheeses, and some celery sticks. She handed the plate to her husband, who greedily bit into a croquette. Vledder returned to his seat with a plate full of food.

DeKok finished his croquette, while Vledder placed the plate with food on his own side table and took another sip of cognac. When he replaced his glass on the table, his face grew serious.

"I was right there on the Kemner Dunes and saw everything happen, but I still don't understand the connections."

DeKok leaned back.

"I'll have to admit that at first I, too, was groping in the dark. It all seemed so ... chaotic, a game without rules. I knew I could easily become confused unless I could find something solid. In the end it came down to Marlies van Haesbergen. She spoke the truth and her recollection was accurate. She *had* seen a dead Vreeden."

"Surely that wasn't it?"

"Of course, not," smiled DeKok. "But her conviction became mine. I had to know why everyone was trying to convince me that a dead Vreeden was alive and on vacation in the Bahamas? One milepost was learning Xaveria Breerode was going to inherit his entire fortune."

"That I can't follow."

DeKok sighed and refilled his glass. He held the bottle up for Vledder with a question in his eyes. Vledder nodded and DeKok leaned forward and refilled the glass that Vledder held out. He looked at his wife. She shook her head.

"Stay where you are. I'll have a sherry."

"You see," said DeKok, after he had replaced the bottle, "almost all of Vreeden's fortune was invested in his dredging company. If Vreeden were to die, the directors would be obliged to liquidate the company and turn all the cash proceeds over to the beneficiary, Ms. Breerode."

"Aha," exclaimed Vledder. "As long as he wasn't officially dead, the money would stay in the company."

"And who benefited in *that* case?"

"Grauw and Middelkoop would have benefited, more than anyone else. They could continue to operate as if nothing had happened."

"Exactly."

"But I haven't got it all, yet," said Vledder. "What about the kidnapping?"

"Our lives," he began in a didactic tone, "are often influenced by sudden feelings of sympathy, or antipathy. It does not matter how one knows about the character of people, human behavior is too complex to predict. How else can one explain the feelings of sympathy Vreeden had for Grauw? Vreeden met Grauw over three years ago in a train. It was the Lorelei Express from Düsseldorf. Grauw had a few convictions behind him for fraud. Why Vreeden, on the briefest acquaintance, decided to take Grauw into his company will always remain a mystery.

Perhaps Vreeden saw in the fast talking, edgy, Mr. Grauw a possible partner. He may have acted out of fatigue, his judgment dulled by weeks of intricate negotiations in Germany. We'll never know."

DeKok paused and nibbled some food. He poured another glass of cognac.

"That's the last one," cautioned his wife. "I'm going to make coffee."

"Yes, dear," said DeKok to her back, as she disappeared toward the kitchen.

Vledder grinned and shook his head as DeKok held up the bottle.

"I'll wait for coffee, thanks. But go on with your story."

"Very well. Grauw soon discovered the backbone of the firm was Vreeden's expertise, business acumen, and fortune. The fortune was too tempting a target for Grauw. Here's how a career swindler operates. Grauw's first act was to isolate his victim by introducing him to Xaveria Breerode. Breerode and Grauw had a history. She had played hostess to prospective victims of his previous swindles."

"So, she has a past also?"

"Of course, everybody has a past."

"Not everyone has a criminal past."

"Yes, yes. Are you going to let me finish?"

"Sorry," said Vledder soothingly. "Go on."

"While in the Haarlem jail for one of his crimes, Grauw met Johan Mindere. Grauw made it possible for Johan to be hired as a butler by Vreeden. When Vreeden bought the estate in Ireland, Grauw wanted to have a trustworthy person in place there. Johan recommended his half-brother, Handsome Karl, as caretaker for the estate."

DeKok drained the last of his glass of cognac. His hand hovered over the bottle, but he resisted the temptation.

"All clear, so far?" he asked.

Vledder nodded.

But I haven't heard a thing about the planned kidnapping."

"No, that's still in the future. The cards had been shuffled. Grauw had set out his net and started to consider plans to get at the loot. But something happened that he had not planned. Vreeden, a confirmed bachelor, fell in love. With Xaveria he found honest affection, sensitivity, and concern for his welfare. Her devotion overwhelmed him. He contacted the notary and had her checked out. The result was a cursory investigation with a meaningless report. He decided to make a will."

Mrs. DeKok returned with a tray, carrying a coffeepot, cups, saucers, cream, and sugar. She arranged it on the sideboard and took a seat.

"When Grauw learned of it," continued DeKok, "he was furious. He contacted Xaveria, but she made it clear she would have nothing to do with him. She let him know, in the event of Vreeden's death, he need not expect anything from her. She even threatened if Grauw continued to bother her, she would speak out about his past. She would also inform Vreeden of his scheming."

"Nice girl," grinned Vledder.

DeKok ignored the remark.

"Grauw discussed the shift in Xaveria's loyalty with Johan Mindere. Together they planned a new approach."

"The kidnapping."

"Yes," nodded DeKok. "Typical of Grauw it was actually a twist on a kidnapping. To deflect any suspicion toward Johan, the plan was to overpower him as well. Paul Vreeden would be kidnapped with his loyal butler. The anonymous kidnapper would demand an enormous ransom. Grauw and Middelkoop would have to decide whether to pay. Grauw knew he could control Middelkoop. He had caught the man in shady practices, payoffs from subcontractors, for instance. Grauw planned to pay the ransom, in order to divert a large portion of Vreeden's fortune to the conspirators ... the butler and Grauw."

"So Xaveria had nothing to do with it?"

"No, she was innocent. For the actual kidnapping, Johan called his half-brother back from Ireland. They agreed on a mobile hiding place. That's how they picked Archie, because he was an accomplished carpenter and would be able to soundproof the boat."

"It all fits nicely together ... now," smirked Vledder.

"But we're not there yet," cautioned DeKok. "Everything was set when Grauw ran into his second complication. Shortly before the kidnapping was to take place, Vreeden suddenly died. He collapsed during a routine business meeting in the company boardroom. He and Middelkoop decided to summon Dr. Haanstra. He could only diagnose the fatal heart attack."

Vledder gripped his head in mock despair.

"All for nothing ... the money was going to Xaveria."

DeKok leaned back in his chair and gratefully accepted a cup of coffee from his wife. Next she served Vledder. Taking a cup of coffee for herself, she reseated herself. Thoughtfully DeKok stirred his coffee.

"We're almost there," he said tiredly. "Grauw's criminal mind was working overtime. He came to what I call a variation on murder."

"Variation?" asked Vledder, puzzled.

"A murderer victimizes someone who is living, someone he wants dead. Grauw, however, wanted to make a dead man live."

"What did he hope to gain?"

"You'd have to think like a criminal. Grauw knew how difficult it is to prove death, absent credible witnesses and a body. That's why someone at the hotel in the Bahamas told Xaveria that Vreeden had left for an unknown destination and had left no forwarding address. Vreeden would go missing and it would take a long time, at least seven years in the Netherlands, before he could be declared legally dead. All that time Xaveria would be unable to inherit. Grauw would have plenty of time to milk the finances of the company for his own benefit."

"What a conniving monster," commented Mrs. DeKok.

"But what about Dr. Haanstra?" Vledder wanted to know.

"Grauw found a way to use him, too. First he impressed on the good doctor the prudence of keeping Paul Vreeden's death to himself. He ordered Haanstra to destroy all his records of Vreeden. When Haanstra reluctantly agreed, Grauw had him—he was Grauw's accomplice. Middelkoop went to the Bahamas, posing as Vreeden. He returned almost immediately after you spoke with him by telephone. Meanwhile Grauw had contacted Johan, ordering him to make Paul Vreeden's body disappear. Johan was reluctant to take on the job and sub-contracted it to his half-brother. Handsome Karl enlisted the help of Black Archie. The rest you know."

"Yes, I imagine Karl liquidated Archie as a dangerous witness. It seems poetic justice for Johan to murder Karl in the place where he'd buried Archie. That leaves Dr. Haanstra—what happened there?"

"I'm afraid," said DeKok morosely, "I may have had a hand in his demise. After I visited Haanstra, he became nervous. He called Grauw to let him know the police had been asking questions. Grauw was not positive of the doctor's reliability and had him murdered to ensure his silence."

DeKok gave a tired smile.

"This morning, early, Fred Prins and I arrested Grauw and Middelkoop, after confronting them with the facts. Middelkoop immediately confessed to his involvement. But I had to confront Grauw with Johan at Warmoes Street. It took a half hour or so, but he confessed to all the charges. The charges include attempt to defraud, attempt to kidnap, attempt to commit murder, conspiracy to commit murder. The beat goes on. The judge advocate is still compiling a list of all the possible charges."

"A good case, a solid solution," commented Vledder.

"Yes, but it would all have fallen apart without the body of Paul Vreeden." He smiled wanly. "I must say never before have I so intensely wanted to find a corpse."

Appendix

(Publisher's Note)

A number of readers have asked questions about *bargoens*, the language of the Dutch underworld and the gutter. In the Inspector DeKok series, Little Lowee speaks almost exclusively in bargoens. To illustrate some of the peculiarities of the language and to illustrate the difficulty of translating the flavor into any other language, the translator has compiled a sample list of some bargoens words and expressions.

Bargoens	Dutch	English
biskoepee	drukte	ado/hubbub
Bokkeslingers	Mariniers	Marines
brooche	voorspoed	prosperity
chateisum	schorem	riffraff
fladder	courant	newspaper
gabber	medeplichtige	partner in crime
geilink	portie	portion
gekat	afgekeurd	disapproved
geknarst	gestrafd	punished
glimmerikke	ogen	eyes
grandige	politieman	police officer
kasafies	papieren	papers (IDs)
kezeire	ziekte	malady
kieskaas	straat hoeren	street whores
knekelmijn	kerkhof	cemetery
koole	spoortrein	railroad

Bargoens	Dutch	English
kooter	kind	child
koudje	mes	knife
kover	fatsoen	decency
lampe lope	betrapt worden	caught in the act
nekeiwe	vrouw	woman
niegus	geluk	luck
niese	vriendin	girlfriend
oksenaar	horloge	watch
Oliekonteland	Brabant	Brabant
ome kolenbrander	hoofd cipier	warden
peiger	dood	dead
planjere	huilen	crying
prinsemarij	politie	police
rag monus	het beste	good luck
sawi	verstand	understanding
sjaakies	bedaard	calm
sjat	betekend	means
slang	ketting	chain
snabbel	fortuin	fortune
snabbeltje	klein fortuin	small fortune
tameier	prostitue	prostitute
Tofelemoons	Roman Katoliek	Roman Catholic
triefel	vuilak (verrader)	filthy person (traitor)
tuimele	inklimmen	breaking in
van de kist	drunken	drunk

ABOUT THE AUTHOR

A. C. Baantjer is the most widely read author in the Netherlands. A former detective inspector of the Amsterdam police, his fictional characters reflect the depth and personality of individuals encountered during his near forty-year career in law enforcement.

Baantjer was honored with the first-ever Master Prize of the Society of Dutch-language Crime Writers. He was also recently knighted by the Dutch monarchy for his lifetime achievements.

The sixty crime novels featuring Inspector Detective DeKok written by Baantjer have achieved a large following among readers in the Netherlands. A television series, based on these novels, reaches an even wider Dutch audience. Launched nearly a decade ago, the 100th episode of the "Baantjer" series recently aired on Dutch channel RTL4.

In large part due to the popularity of the televised "Baantjer" series, sales of Baantjer's novels have increased significantly over the past several years. In 2001, the five millionth copy of his books was sold—a number never before reached by a Dutch author.

Known as the "Dutch Conan Doyle," Baantjer's following continues to grow and conquer new territory. According to the Netherlands Library Information Service, a single copy of a Baanjter title is checked out of a library more than 700,000 times a year.

The DeKok series has been published in China, Russia, Korea, and throughout Europe. Speck Press is pleased to bring you clear and invigorating translations to the English language.

INSPECTOR DEKOK SERIES
BY BAANTJER

DEKOK AND THE GEESE OF DEATH
Renowned Amsterdam mystery author Baantjer brings to life
Inspector DeKok in another stirring potboiler full of suspenseful
twists and unusual conclusions.
ISBN: 0-9725776-6-1, ISBN13: 978-0-9725776-6-3

DEKOK AND MURDER BY MELODY
"Death is entitled to our respect," says Inspector DeKok who finds
himself once again amidst dark dealings. A triple murder in the
Amsterdam Concert Gebouw has him unveiling the truth behind
two dead ex-junkies and their housekeeper.
ISBN: 0-9725776-9-6, ISBN13: 978-0-9725776-9-4

DEKOK AND THE DEATH OF A CLOWN
A high-stakes jewel theft and a dead clown blend into a single riddle
for Inspector DeKok to solve. The connection of the crimes at
first eludes him
ISBN: 1-933108-03-7, ISBN13: 978-1-933108-03-2

DEKOK AND MURDER BY INSTALLMENT
Although at first it seemed to be a case for the narcotics division, it
soon evolves into a series of sinister and almost impossible murders.
Never before have DeKok and Vledder been so involved in a case
whereby murder, drug smuggling, and child prostitution are almost
daily occurences.
ISBN: 1-933108-07-X, ISBN13: 978-1-933108-07-0

Boost

by Steve Brewer

Sam Hill steals cars. Not just any cars, but collectible cars, rare works of automotive artistry. Sam's a specialist, and he's made a good life for himself.

But things change after he steals a primo 1965 Thunderbird. In the trunk, Sam finds a corpse, a police informant with a bullet hole between his eyes. Somebody set Sam up. Played a trick on him. And Sam, a prankster himself, can't let it go. He must get his revenge with an even bigger practical joke, one that soon has gangsters gunning for him and police on his tail.

"… entertaining, amusing … . This tightly plotted crime novel packs in a lot of action as it briskly moves along."
—*Chicago Tribune*

"Brewer earns four stars for a clever plot, totally engaging characters, and a pay-back ending … ."
—*Mystery Scene*

ISBN: 1-933108-02-9 | ISBN13: 978-1-933108-02-5

Killing Neptune's Daughter

by Randall Peffer

Returning to his hometown was something Billy Bagwell always dreaded. But he felt he owed it to Tina, the object of his childhood sexual obsession, to see her off properly. Even in death she could seduce him to her. Upon his return to Wood's Hole on Cape Cod, Billy's past with his old friends—especially his best friend, present day Catholic priest Zal—floods his mind with classic machismo and rite-of-passage boyhood events. But some of their moments were a bit darker, and all seemed to revolve around or involve Tina … moments that Billy didn't want to remember.

This psycho-thriller carries Billy deeper and deeper into long-repressed memories of thirty-five-year-old crimes. As the days grow darker, Billy finds himself caught in a turbulent tide of past homoerotic encounters, lost innocence, rage, religion, and lust.

"… the perfect book for those who fancy the darker, grittier side of mystery. A hit-you-in-the-guts psychothriller, this is a compelling story of one man's search for truth and inner peace."
—*Mystery Scene*

ISBN: 0-9725776-5-3 | ISBN13: 978-1-933108-05-6

Nick Madrid Mysteries
by Peter Guttridge

No Laughing Matter

Tom Sharpe meets Raymond Chandler in this humorous
and brilliant debut. Meet Nick Madrid and the "Bitch of the
Broadsheets," Bridget Frost, as they trail a killer from Montreal to
Edinburgh to the ghastly lights of Hollywood.
ISBN: 0-9725776-4-5, ISBN13: 978-0-9725776-4-9

A Ghost of a Chance

New Age meets the Old Religion as Nick is bothered and
bewildered by pagans, satanists, and metaphysicians. Seances, sabbats,
a horse-ride from hell, and a kick-boxing zebra all come Nick's way
as he tracks a treasure once in the possession of Aleister Crowley.
ISBN: 0-9725776-8-8, ISBN13: 978-0-9725776-8-7

Two to Tango

On a trip down the Amazon, journalist Nick Madrid survives
kidnapping, piranhas, and urine-loving fish that lodge where a man
least wants one lodged. After those heroics, Nick joins up with a
Rock Against Drugs tour where he finds himself tracking down the
would-be killer of the tour's pain-in-the-posterior headliner.
ISBN: 1-933108-00-2, ISBN13: 978-1-933108-00-1

The Once and Future Con

Avalon theme parks and medieval Excaliburger banquets are the last
things journalist Nick Madrid expects to find when he arrives at
what is supposedly the grave of the legendary King Arthur. As Nick
starts to dig around for an understanding, it isn't Arthurian relics, but
murder victims that he uncovers.
ISBN: 1-933108-06-1, ISBN13: 978-1-933108-06-3

Peter Guttridge is the Royal Literary Fund Writing Fellow at Southampton University and teaches creative writing. Between 1998 and 2002 he was the director of the Brighton Literature Festival. As a freelance journalist he has written about literature, film, and comedy for a range of British newspapers and magazines. Since 1998 he has been the mystery reviewer for *The Observer*, one of Britain's most prestigious Sunday newspapers. He also writes about—and doggedly practices—astanga vinyasa yoga.

Praise for the Nick Madrid Mysteries

"Highly recommended."
—*Library Journal*, starred review

"… I couldn't put it down. This is classic Guttridge, with all the humor I've come to expect from the series. Nick is a treasure, and Bridget a good foil to his good nature."
—*Deadly Pleasures*

"Guttridge's series is among the funniest and sharpest in the genre, with a level of intelligence often lacking in better-known fare."
—*Baltimore Sun*

"… one of the most engaging novels of 2005. Highly entertaining … this is humor wonderfully combined with mystery."
—*Foreword*

" … Peter Guttridge is off to a rousing start … a serious contender in the mystery genre."
—*Chicago Tribune*

"[The] Nick Madrid mysteries are nothing if not addictively, insanely entertaining … but what's really important is the mix of good suspense, fast-and-furious one-liners and impeccable slapstick."
—*Ruminator*

"… both funny and clever. This is one of the funniest mysteries to come along in quite a while."
—*Mystery Scene*

For a complete catalog of our books please contact us at:

speck press
po box 102004
denver, co 80250, usa
e: books@speckpress.com
t & f: 800-996-9783
w: speckpress.com

Our books are available through your local bookseller.